"I'm not b⟨ P9-BIT-681
blaming the situation." His
eyes met hers and she saw
something that stunned her for
a second. Was that concern?

"If you needed money, you should have
come to me," he said with dictatorial
authority, and she knew she'd made a
stupid mistake. That wasn't concern. It
was contempt.

"There was no need for you to become a
stripper," he remarked.

Her heart stopped, and the blush blazed
like wildfire.

Had he just said stripper?

He cupped her cheek. The unexpected
contact made her outraged reply stick in
her throat.

"I know things ended badly between us,
but we were friends once. I can help you."
His thumb skimmed across her cheek with
the lightest of touches. "And whatever
happens, you're finding another job." The
patronizing tone did nothing to diminish
the arousal darkening his eyes. "Because,
quite apart from anything else, you're a
terrible stripper."

HEIDI RICE was born and bred and still lives in London, England. She has two boys who love to bicker, a wonderful husband who, luckily for everyone, has loads of patience, and a supportive and ever-growing British/French/Irish/American family. As much as Heidi adores "the Big Smoke," she also loves America, and every two years or so she and her best friend leave hubby and kids behind and *Thelma and Louise* it across the States for a couple of weeks (although they always leave out the driving-off-a-cliff bit). She's been a film buff since her early teens, and a romance junkie for almost as long. She indulged her first love by being a film reviewer for ten years. Then two years ago she decided to spice up her life by writing romance. Discovering the fantastic sisterhood of romance writers (both published and unpublished) in Britain and America made it a wild and wonderful journey to her first Harlequin novel, and she's looking forward to many more to come.

UNFINISHED BUSINESS WITH THE DUKE

HEIDI RICE

~ Back in His Bed ~

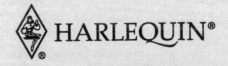

HARLEQUIN®

TORONTO • NEW YORK • LONDON
AMSTERDAM • PARIS • SYDNEY • HAMBURG
STOCKHOLM • ATHENS • TOKYO • MILAN • MADRID
PRAGUE • WARSAW • BUDAPEST • AUCKLAND

Recycling programs
for this product may
not exist in your area.

ISBN-13: 978-0-373-52788-5

UNFINISHED BUSINESS WITH THE DUKE

First North American Publication 2010.

www.eHarlequin.com

Printed in U.S.A.

UNFINISHED BUSINESS WITH THE DUKE

A special thanks to my Florentine specialists,
Steve and Biz, to Katherine at the terrific
King's Head Theatre in Islington,
and Leonardo, who answered my daft
questions about architecture.

CHAPTER ONE

THE six-inch stiletto heels of Issy Helligan's thigh-high leather boots echoed like gunshots against the marble floor of the gentlemen's club. The sharp rhythmic cracks sounded like a firing squad doing target practice as she approached the closed door at the end of the corridor.

How appropriate.

She huffed and came to a stop. The gunshots cut off, but her stomach carried right on going, doing a loop-the-loop and then swaying like the pendulum of Big Ben. Recognising the symptoms of chronic stage fright, Issy pressed her palm to her midriff as she focussed on the elaborate brass plaque announcing the entrance to the 'East Wing Common Room'.

Calm down. You can do this. You're a theatrical professional with seven years' experience.

Detecting the muffled rumble of loud male laughter, she locked her knees as a thin trickle of sweat ran down her back beneath her second-hand Versace mac.

People are depending on you. People you care about. Getting ogled by a group of pompous old fossils is a small price to pay for keeping those people gainfully employed.

It was a mantra she'd been repeating for the past hour—to absolutely no avail.

After grappling with the knot on the mac's belt, she pulled the coat off and placed it on the upholstered chair beside the door. Then she looked down at her costume—and Big Ben's pendulum got stuck in her throat.

Blood-red satin squeezed her ample curves into an hourglass shape, making her cleavage look like a freak of nature. She took a shallow breath and the bustier's underwiring dug into her ribs.

She tugged the band out of her hair and let the mass of Pre-Raphaelite curls tumble over her bare shoulders as she counted to ten.

Fine, so the costume from last season's production of *The Rocky Horror Picture Show* wasn't exactly subtle, but she hadn't had a lot of options at such short notice—and the man who had booked her that morning hadn't wanted subtle.

'Tarty, darling. That's the look I'm after,' he'd stated in his cut-glass Etonian accent. 'Rodders is moving to Dubai and we plan to show him what he'll be missing. So don't stint on the T and A, sweetheart.'

It had been on the tip of Issy's tongue to tell him to buzz off and hire himself a stripper, but then he'd mentioned the astronomical sum he was prepared to pay if she 'put on a decent show'—and her tongue had gone numb.

After six months of scrimping and saving and struggling to find a sponsor, Issy was fast running out of ways to get the thirty grand she needed to keep the Crown and Feathers Theatre Pub open for another season. The Billet Doux Singergram Agency had been the jewel in the crown of her many fund-raising ideas. But so far they'd had a grand total of six bookings—and all of those had been from well-meaning friends. Having worked her way up from general dogsbody to general manager in the last seven years, she had everyone at the theatre looking to her to make sure the show went on.

Issy sighed, the weight of responsibility making her head hurt as the corset's whalebone panels constricted around her lungs. With the bank threatening to foreclose on the theatre's loan any minute, feminist principles were just another of the luxuries she could no longer afford.

When she'd taken the booking eight hours ago she'd been determined to see it as a golden opportunity. She'd do a tastefully suggestive rendition of 'Life Is a Cabaret', flash a modest amount of T and A and walk away with a nice healthy sum to add to the Crown and Feathers's survival kitty, plus the possibility of some serious word-of-mouth business. After all, this was one of the most exclusive gentlemen's clubs in the world, boasting princes, dukes and lords of the realm, not to mention Europe's richest and most powerful businessmen among its membership.

Really, it should be a doddle. She'd made it quite clear to her booker what a singing telegram did—and did not—entail. And Roderick Carstairs and his mates couldn't possibly be as tough an audience to crack as the twenty-two five-year-olds tripping on a sugar rush she'd sung 'Happy Birthday' to last week.

Or so she hoped.

But as Issy eased the heavy oak panelled door to the East Wing Common Room open, and heard the barrage of male hoots and guffaws coming from inside, that hope died a quick and painful death.

From the sound of it, her audience were primed and ready for her—and not nearly as old and fossilised as she'd assumed. The corset squeezed her ribcage as she stayed rooted in the doorway, shielded from view.

Putting on 'a decent show' didn't seem such a doddle any more.

She was staring blankly at the rows of bookcases lining the wall, mustering the courage to walk into the lions' den, when she caught a movement on the balcony opposite. Silhouetted by the dusky evening light, a tall figure strode into view, talking into his mobile phone. It was impossible to make out his features, but *déjà vu* had the hair on the back of Issy's neck standing to attention. Momentarily transfixed by the stranger's broad-shouldered build, and the forceful, predatory way he moved in the small space, Issy shivered, thinking of a tiger prowling a cage.

She jumped at the disembodied chorus of rowdy masculine cheers and dragged her gaze away.

Focus, Issy, focus.

She straightened her spine and took a step forward, but then her eyes darted to the balcony again. The stranger had stopped moving. Was he watching her?

She thought of the tiger again. And then memory blindsided her.

'Gio,' she whispered, as her breath clogged in her lungs and the corset constricted like a vice around her torso.

She gasped in a breath as heat seared up the back of her neck and made her scalp burn.

Ignore him.

She pulled her gaze away, mortified that the mere thought of Giovanni Hamilton still made all her erogenous zones do the happy dance and her heart squeeze painfully in her chest.

Don't be ridiculous.

That guy could not be Gio. She couldn't possibly be that unlucky. To come face to face with the biggest disaster of her life when she was about to waltz into another. Clearly stress was making her hallucinate.

Issy pushed her shoulders back and took as deep a breath as the corset's stays would allow.

Enough with the nervous breakdown, already. It's showtime.

Striding into the main body of the room, she launched into the sultry opening bars of Liza Minnelli's signature song. Only to come to a stumbling halt, her stomach lurching back into Big Ben mode, as she rounded the door and got an eyeful of Rodders and his mates. The mob of young, debauched and completely pie-eyed Hooray Henries lunged to their feet, jeers and wolf whistles echoing off the antique furnishings as the room erupted.

Issy's throat constricted in horror as she imagined Little Red Riding Hood being fed to a pack of sex-starved, booze-sodden wolves while singing a show tune in her underwear.

Suddenly a firing squad looked remarkably appealing.

Go ahead and shoot me now, fellas.

What in God's name was Issy Helligan doing working as a stripper?

Gio Hamilton stood in the shadows of the balcony, stunned into silence, his gaze fixed on the young woman who strutted into the room with the confidence of a courtesan. Her full figure moved in time with her long, leggy strides. Sequins glittered on an outfit that would make a hooker blush.

'Gio?' The heavily accented voice of his partnership manager crackled down the phone from Florence.

'*Si, Gio.*' He pressed the phone to his ear and tried to

get his mind to engage. 'I'll get back to you about the Venice project,' he said, slipping into English. 'You know how the Italian authorities love red tape—it's probably just a formality. *Ciao*.' He disconnected the call—and stared.

That couldn't be the sweet, impulsive and impossibly naïve girl he'd grown up with. Could it?

But then he noticed the pale freckled skin on her shoulder blades and he knew. Heat pulsed in his groin as he recalled Issy the last time he'd seen her—that same pale skin flushed pink by their recent lovemaking and those wild auburn curls cascading over bare shoulders.

The smoky, seductive notes of an old theatre song, barely audible above the hoots and jeers, yanked Gio out of the past and brought him slap-bang up to date. Issy's rich, velvety voice sent shivers rippling up his spine and arousal flared—before the song was drowned out by the chant of 'Get it off!' from Carstairs and his crowd.

Gio's contempt for the arrogant toff and his cronies turned to disgust as Issy's singing stopped and she froze. Suddenly she wasn't the inexperienced young temptress who'd seduced him one hot summer night, but the awkward girl who had trailed after him throughout his teenage years, her bright blue eyes glowing with adoration.

He stuffed his phone into his back pocket, anger and arousal and something else he didn't want to acknowledge coiling in his gut.

Then Carstairs lunged. Gio's fingers clenched into fists as the younger man grabbed Issy around the waist. Her head twisted to avoid the boozy kiss.

To hell with that.

The primitive urge to protect came from nowhere.

'Get your filthy hands off her, Carstairs.'

The shout echoed as eleven pairs of eyes turned his way.

Issy yelped as he strode towards her, those exotic turquoise eyes going wide with astonishment and then blank with shock.

Carstairs raised his head, his ruddy face glazed with champagne and confusion. 'Who the…?'

Gio slammed an upper-cut straight into the idiot's jaw. Pain ricocheted up his arm.

'Ow! Dammit,' he breathed, cradling his throbbing knuckles as he watched Carstairs crumple onto the carpet.

Hearing Issy's sharp gasp, he looked round to see her eyes roll back. He caught her as she flopped, and scooped her into his arms. Carrying her against his chest, he tuned out the shouts and taunts coming from Carstairs's friends. Not one of them was sober enough—or had enough gumption—to cause him a problem.

'Kick this piece of rubbish out of here when he comes to,' Gio said to the elderly attendant who had scurried in from his post in the billiards room next door.

The old guy bobbed his head. 'Yes, Your Grace. Will the lady be all right?'

'She'll be fine. Once you've dealt with Carstairs, have some ice water and brandy sent to my suite.'

He drew a deep breath as he strolled down the corridor towards the lifts, caught the rose scent of Issy's shampoo and realised it wasn't only his knuckles throbbing.

He gave the attendant a stiff nod as he walked into the lift, with Issy still out cold in his arms. She stirred slightly and he got his first good look at her face in the fluorescent light.

He could see the tantalising sprinkle of freckles on her nose. And the slight overbite which gave her lips an irresistible pout. Despite the heavy stage make-up and the glossy coating of letterbox-red lipstick, her heart-shaped face still had the tantalising combination of innocence and sensuality that had caused him so many sleepless nights a lifetime ago.

Gio's gaze strayed to the swell of her cleavage, barely confined by dark red satin. The antique lift shuddered to a stop at his floor, and his groin began to throb in earnest.

He adjusted her dead weight, flexing his shoulder muscles as he headed down the corridor to the suite of rooms he kept at the club.

Even at seventeen Issy Helligan had been a force of nature. As impossible to ignore as she was to control. He was a man who loved taking risks, but Issy had still been able to shock the hell out of him.

From the looks of things that hadn't changed.

He shoved opened the door to his suite, and walked through into the bedroom. Placing his cargo on the bed, he stepped back and stared at her barely clad body in the half-light.

So what did he do with her now?

He hadn't a clue where the urge to ride to her rescue had come from. But giving Carstairs a right jab and knocking the drunken idiot out cold was where any lingering sense of responsibility both started and stopped. He was nobody's knight in shining armour.

He frowned, his irritation rising right alongside his arousal as he watched her shallow breathing.

What was that thing made of? Armour-plating? No

wonder she'd fainted. It looked as if she was struggling to take a decent breath.

Cursing softly, he perched on the edge of the bed and tugged the bow at her cleavage. Issy gave a soft moan as the satin knot slipped. He loosened the laces, his eyes riveted to the plump flesh of her breasts as the corset expanded.

She was even more exquisite than he remembered.

The pain in his crotch increased, but he resisted the urge to loosen the contraption further and expose her to his gaze. Then he spotted the red marks on her pale skin where the panels had dug into tender flesh.

'For heaven's sake, Issy,' he whispered as he smoothed his thumb over the bruising.

What had she been thinking, wearing this outfit in the first place? And then prancing around in front of a drunken fool like Carstairs?

Issy Helligan had always needed a keeper. He'd have to give her a good talking-to when she came round.

He stood and walked to the window. After flinging open the velvet drapes, he sat in the gilt chair beside the bed. This shouldn't be too hard to sort out.

The reason for her disastrous charade downstairs had to be something to do with money. Issy had always been headstrong and foolhardy, but she'd never been promiscuous. So he'd offer her an injection of capital when she woke up.

She'd never have to do anything this reckless again— and he'd be free to forget about her.

His gaze drifted to the tantalising glimpse of one rosy nipple peeking over the satin rim of the corset.

And if she knew what was good for her, she'd damn well take the money.

Issy's eyelids fluttered as she inhaled the fresh scent of clean linen.

'Hello again, Isadora.' The low, masculine voice rumbled across her consciousness and made her insides feel deliciously warm and fuzzy.

She took a deep breath and sighed. Hallelujah. She could breathe. The relief was intoxicating.

'Mmm? What?' she purred. She felt as if she were floating on a cloud. A light, fluffy cloud made of delicious pink candyfloss.

'I loosened your torture equipment. No wonder you fainted. You could barely breathe.'

It was the gorgeous voice again, crisp British vowels underlaid with a lazy hint of the Mediterranean—and a definite hint of censure. Issy frowned. Didn't she know that voice?

Her eyes opened, and she stared at an elaborate plaster moulding on the ceiling. Swivelling her head, she saw a man by her bedside. Her first thought was that he looked far too masculine for the fancy gilt chair. But then she focussed on his face, and the bolt of recognition hit her, knocking her off the candyfloss cloud and shoving her head first into sticky reality.

She snapped her eyelids shut, threw one arm over her face and sank back down into the pillows. 'Go away. You're a hallucination,' she groaned. But it was too late.

Even the brief glimpse had seared the image of his harsh, handsome features onto her retinas and made her heartbeat hit panic mode. The sculpted cheekbones, the square jaw with a small dent in the chin, the wavy chestnut hair pushed back from dark brows and those thickly-lashed chocolate eyes more tempting than original sin. Pain lanced into her chest as she recalled how those eyes had looked the last time she'd seen them, shadowed with annoyance and regret.

Then everything else came flooding back. And Issy groaned louder.

Carstairs's sweaty hands gripping her waist, the rank whiff of whisky and cigars on his breath, the pulse of fear replaced by shock as Carstairs's head snapped back and Gio loomed over her. Then the deafening buzzing in her ears before she'd done her 'Perils of Pauline' act.

No way. This could not be happening. Gio had to be a hallucination.

'Leave me alone and let me die in peace,' she moaned.

She heard a husky chuckle and grimaced. Had she said that out loud?

'Once a drama queen, always a drama queen, I see, Isadora?'

She dropped her arm and stared at her tormentor. Taking in the tanned biceps stretching the sleeves of his black polo shirt and the teasing glint in his eyes, she resigned herself to the fact this was no hallucination. The few strands of silver at his temples and the crinkles around the corners of his eyes hadn't been there ten years ago, but at thirty-one Giovanni Hamilton was as devastatingly gorgeous as he had been at twenty-one—and twice as much of a hunk.

Why couldn't he have got fat, bald and ugly? It was the least he deserved.

'Don't call me Isadora. I hate that name,' she said, not caring if she sounded snotty.

'Really?' One eyebrow rose in mocking enquiry as his lips quirked. 'Since when?'

Since you walked away.

She quashed the sentimental thought. To think she'd once adored it when he'd called her by her given name. Had often basked for days in the proof that he'd noticed her.

How pitiful.

Luckily she wasn't that needy, eager-to-please teenager any more.

'Since I grew up and decided it didn't suit me,' she said, pretending not to notice the warm liquid sensation turning her insides to mush as he smiled at her.

The eyebrow rose another notch and the sexy grin widened as he lounged in his chair. He didn't look the least bit wounded by her rebuff.

His gaze dipped to her cleavage. 'I can see how grown up you are. It's kind of hard to miss.'

Heat sizzled at the suggestive tone. She bolted upright, aware of how much flesh she had on display as the bustier drooped. She drew her knees up and wrapped her arms around her shins as the brutal blush fanned out across her chest.

'I was on a job,' she said defensively, annoyed that the costume felt more revealing now than it had in front of Carstairs and all his mates.

'A job? Is that what you call it?' Gio commented dryly. 'What sort of *job* requires you to get assaulted by an idiot like Carstairs?' His eyes narrowed. 'What exactly do you think would have happened if I hadn't been there?'

She heard the sanctimonious note of disapproval—
and the injustice of the accusation made her want to
scream.

In hindsight, she should never have accepted the
booking. And maybe it had been a mistake to walk into
that room once she'd known how plastered her audience
was. But she'd been under so much pressure for months
now. Her livelihood and the livelihood of people she
loved was at stake.

So she'd taken a chance. A stupid, desperate, foolish
chance that had backfired spectacularly. But she wasn't
going to regret it. And she certainly wasn't going to be
criticised for it by someone who had never cared about
anyone in his entire life but himself.

'Don't you *dare* imply I'm to blame for Carstairs's
appalling behaviour,' she said, fury making the words
louder than she'd intended.

Surprise flickered in Gio's eyes.

Good.

It was about time he realised she wasn't the simper-
ing little groupie she'd once been.

'The man was blind drunk and a lech,' she continued,
shuffling over to the other side of the bed and swinging
her legs to the floor. 'Nobody asked you to get involved.'
She stood and faced him. 'You did that all on your own.
I would have been perfectly fine if you hadn't been
there.'

Probably.

She marched across the lavishly furnished bedroom—
keeping a death grip on the sagging costume. What she
wouldn't give right now to be wearing her favourite jeans
and a T-shirt. Somehow her speech didn't have as much

impact while she was dressed like an escapee from the
Moulin Rouge.

'Where do you think you're going?' he said, his voice
dangerously low.

'I'm leaving,' she replied, reaching for the doorknob.

But as she yanked the door, all set to make a grand
exit, a large, tanned hand slapped against the wood
above her head and slammed it shut.

'No, you're not,' he said.

She whipped round and immediately realised her
mistake. Her breath caught as her bare shoulders butted
the door. He stood so close she could see the flecks of
gold in his irises, taste the spicy scent of his aftershave,
and feel the heat of his body inches from hers.

She clasped her arms over her chest as her nipples
puckered, awareness making every one of her pulse-
points pound.

'What?' she snapped, cornered. The last time she'd
been this close to Gio she'd been losing her virginity to
him.

'There's no need to go storming off.' The rock-hard
bicep next to her ear tensed before his arm dropped to
his side. Her breath released in an audible puff as he
eased back.

'You misunderstood me,' he said, heaving an impatient sigh.

'About what, exactly?' She tilted her head, thrust
her chin out.

How infuriating.

At five foot six, and with six-inch heels on, she
ought to be able to look him in the eye. No such luck.
Gio had always been tall—tall and lanky—but when
had he got so…solid?

She tried to look bored. No easy feat, given her limited acting skills and the fact that her heart felt as if it were being ripped out of her chest all over again. She pushed the memory back, locking it back in the box marked 'Biggest Mistake of your Life', while his gaze roamed over her, the chocolate-brown giving nothing away. To think she'd once believed that bleak expression was enigmatic, when all it had ever been was proof Gio had no soul.

'Carstairs deserved everything he got, and I enjoyed giving it to him,' he said coldly, shoving a fist into the pocket of his trousers. 'I'm not blaming you. I'm blaming the situation.' His eyes met hers and she saw something that stunned her for a second. Was that concern?

'If you needed money you should have come to me,' he said with dictatorial authority, and she knew she'd made a stupid mistake. That wasn't concern. It was contempt.

'There was no need for you to become a stripper,' he remarked.

Her heart stopped and the blush blazed like wildfire. *Did he just say stripper?*

He cupped her cheek. The unexpected contact had her outraged reply getting stuck in her throat.

'I know things ended badly between us, but we were friends once. I can help you.' His thumb skimmed across her cheek with the lightest of touches. 'And, whatever happens, you're finding another job.' The patronising tone did nothing to diminish the arousal darkening his eyes. 'Because, quite apart from anything else, you're a terrible stripper.'

CHAPTER TWO

Issy wasn't often rendered speechless. As a rule she liked to talk. And she was never shy about voicing her opinion. But right now she couldn't utter a single syllable, because she was far too busy trying to figure out what outraged her the most.

That Gio thought she was a stripper. That he thought she was terrible. That he actually thought it was any of his business. Or that he should have the audacity to claim he had been her friend...

'We're not friends,' she spluttered. 'Not any more. I got over that delusion a long time ago. Remember?'

His hand stroked her nape, making it hard for her to concentrate. 'Perhaps friendship's not the right word.' His eyes met hers, and what she saw made her gasp. His pupils had dilated, the chocolate-brown now black with desire. He was turned on. Seriously turned on. But what shocked her more was the vicious throb of arousal in her own abdomen.

'How about we kiss and make up?' he said, purpose and demand clear in the husky voice.

Before she could respond he brushed his lips across hers, then dipped his head and kissed the swell of her left breast. Raw desire assailed her, paralysing her tongue as he nipped at the sensitive flesh. Her breath gushed out and her head bumped against the door, shock and panic obliterated by the swift jolt of molten heat.

Stop him. Stop this.

The words crashed through her mind. But the only thing that registered was the brutal yearning to feel his mouth on her breast. She could still remember the way his insistent lips had once ignited her senses. Her arms relaxed their death grip on the corset, and the ripe peak spilled out.

She sobbed as he circled the rigid nipple with his tongue, then captured it between his lips and suckled strongly. Vivid memory and raw new sensation tangled as she arched into his mouth. Her thigh muscles clutched and released as she surrendered. He pushed the sagging bodice down, cupped her other breast. She moaned as he tugged at the swelling peak.

The firestorm of need twisted and built. Dazed, she clasped his head, gripping the silky waves—and felt the sharp knock on the door rap against her back.

Her eyes popped open as he raised his head.

'Hell, ten years isn't enough,' he murmured, the sinful chocolate gaze hot with lust and knowledge.

She scrambled away, shame shattering the sensual spell. Drawing in a ragged breath, she grasped the sagging corset, covered herself, wincing as the cool satin touched tender flesh.

The knock sounded again, and panic skittered up her spine.

What had just happened? What had she let happen? How could he still have this effect on her?

'Excuse me, Your Grace.' The tentative voice, muffled by the door, broke the charged silence. 'Would you like me to leave the tray here?'

'Just a minute,' Gio shouted, his eyes fixed on hers. 'Stand over there,' he murmured, nodding to a space behind the door that would keep her out of sight.

She bristled at the note of command, but stepped back. She had to get out of here. Before this got any worse.

'I have your brandy and iced water, Your Grace,' the footman announced as Gio swung open the door. 'And the lady's coat. It was on the hall chair downstairs.'

'Great,' Gio said curtly as he took the coat from unseen hands. Glancing her way, he passed it to her.

She stuffed her arms into the sleeves. Hastily tying the corset laces, she belted the mac as she watched Gio hand over a large tip and take the tray from the invisible footman.

He scowled as he pushed the door shut. 'Let's talk,' he said, sliding the tray onto the table beside the door.

'No, let's not,' she said, pleased that she'd stopped shaking long enough to cover some of her modesty.

She stepped forward and gripped the door handle, but she had wrestled it open less than an inch before his hand slapped against the wood, holding it closed.

'Stop behaving like a child. Surely after ten years you're over that night?'

She flinched at the impatient words. Then straightened, his casual reference to the worse night of her life forcing her pride to finally put in an appearance. Better late than never.

'Of course I'm over it,' she said emphatically, ignoring the ache under her breastbone. 'I'm not a child any more. Or an imbecile.'

She'd rather suffer the tortures of hell than admit

she'd cried herself to sleep for over a month after he'd gone. And lived with that pointless spurt of hope every time the phone rang for much longer. It was pathetic. And all completely academic now.

She might still have a problem controlling her body's reaction to him. But thankfully her heart was safe. She wasn't that overly romantic child any more—who'd believed infatuation was love.

But that didn't mean she was going to forgive him.

'I may have been young and foolish.' She tried not to cringe at the memory of *how* young and foolish. 'But luckily I happen to be a fast learner.'

Fast enough to know she would never fall that easily again. And especially not for a man like Gio, who didn't understand love and had no idea what it was worth.

'What's the problem, then?' He shrugged, as if that night had never happened. 'There's still a powerful attraction between us.' His eyes lowered to her lips. 'The way you just responded to me is proof of that. So why get upset because we acted on it?'

'I'm not upset!' she shouted. She paused, lowered her voice. 'To get upset, I'd actually have to give a damn.'

She turned to make her getaway again, but his hand slammed back against the door.

'Will you stop doing that?' she said, exasperated.

'You're not leaving until we sort out your situation,' he said, with infuriating patience.

'What situation?'

'You know very well what situation.'

His mouth had flattened into a grim line. What on earth was he on about?

'In case you haven't noticed, Your Dukeship, this is a free country. You can't hold me here against my will.'

'Nothing's free—and you know it.' His eyes raked over her outfit. 'Let me spell it out. I'm here in the UK having Hamilton Hall renovated, which means I can transfer the money you need by the end of today.'

What?

Her tongue went numb. Good God, he'd rendered her speechless again.

'And don't tell me you *like* working as a stripper,' he continued, clearly oblivious to her rising outrage, 'because I saw how petrified you were when Carstairs put his paws on you. My guess is this was your first job. And I intend to ensure it's also your last.'

'I'm not a stripper,' she all but choked. Of all the arrogant, patronising, overbearing… 'And even if I were, I would never be desperate enough to ask *you* for help.'

She'd always stood on her own two feet, had worked hard for her independence and was proud of what she'd achieved—even if it *was* all about to belong to the bank.

'If you're not a stripper,' he said, scepticism sharpening his voice, 'then what on earth were you doing downstairs?'

'I was delivering a singing telegram.'

His brow furrowed. 'A what?'

'Never mind.' She waved the question away. Why was she explaining herself to him? 'The point is, I don't need your help.'

'Stop being stupid.' He gripped her arm as she tried to turn. 'Whatever you were doing, it's obvious you must be desperate. I'm offering you a way out here. No strings attached. You'd be a fool not to take it.'

She tried to wrestle free, glaring at him when his fingers only tightened. 'I'd be an even bigger fool to take anything from you.' Anger and humiliation churned, bringing back the feeling of defeat and inadequacy that had dogged her for years after he'd walked away. And she hit back without thinking. 'Haven't you figured it out yet, Gio?' she said, hating the bitterness and negativity in her voice. 'I'd rather do twenty stripteases for Carstairs and his whole entourage than accept a penny from you. I happen to have a few principles, and I would never take money from someone I detest.'

His fingers released as the words struck home.

She fumbled with the door and darted out of the room, determined not to care about the shock on his face.

'Your body may be all grown up, Isadora.' The deep voice taunted her as her booted heels clicked on the polished parquet. 'What a shame the rest of you still has a way to go.'

She squared her shoulders as the door slammed at her back, and plunged her fists into the pockets of the mac, battling the blush burning her scalp. As she rushed down the hallway she played her parting shot over in her mind.

If only she *did* detest him.

Unfortunately, where Gio was concerned, nothing was ever that simple.

Gio strode into the living room of the suite and dumped the tray on the coffee table. Sitting on the fussy Queen Anne chaise-longue, he kicked off his shoes, propped his feet on the equally fussy antique table, and for the first time in years fervently wished for a cigarette.

Reaching for the generous glass of vintage cognac, he chugged it down in one punishing swallow. The burn in his throat did nothing to alleviate the pain in his groin, or the frustration making his head start to throb.

Issy Helligan was a walking disaster area.

He stared at the thick ridge in his trousers.

If that didn't go down in a minute he'd be forced to take a cold shower. Dropping his head against the sofa's backrest, he gazed at the ceiling. When had he last been stuck with an erection this persistent?

The vivid memory of Issy, her lithe young body moulded to his as he rode his motorcycle through the leafy country lanes to the Hall, instantly sprang to mind. And the blood pounded even harder.

Unbelievable. He could still recall every detail of that twenty-minute trip. As if it had happened ten seconds ago instead of ten years. Her full breasts flattening against his back, her thighs hugging his backside, her arms clinging to his waist—and the earlier shock to his system when she'd first strolled out of the school gates and climbed aboard the reconditioned Harley.

He'd expected to see the plump, cute tomboy he remembered—not a statuesque young woman with the face and figure of a goddess.

At twenty-one, he had been far more experienced than most men his age, and lusting after a girl of seventeen—a girl who had once been his only friend—had seemed wrong. But he hadn't been able to control his reaction to her then any more than he had today.

He cursed. If it hadn't been for the footman's well-timed interruption five minutes ago things would have gone a great deal further.

The second his lips had tasted her warm, fragrant flesh, and he'd heard her breath catch and felt her shudder of response, instinct had taken over—as it always did with Issy. His mouth had closed over her breast and he'd revelled in the feel of her nipple swelling and hardening under his tongue.

He blew out a breath and adjusted his trousers.

But Issy had changed. She wasn't the sweet, passionate teenager who had once adored him, but a vibrant, self-aware and stunningly beautiful young woman—who detested him.

Gio placed the brandy glass back on the tray, frustrated by the strange little jolt in his chest. He pressed the heel of his hand against his breastbone. He didn't care what she thought of him. Why should he?

Women tended to overreact about this stuff. Look at most of the women he'd dated.

He always made it crystal-clear he was only interested in recreational sex and lively companionship but they never believed him. And recently the triple whammy of career success, reaching his thirties and inheriting a dukedom had only made them harder to convince.

Angry words had never bothered him before when the inevitable breakup occurred. So why had Issy's?

Gio frowned and pushed the hair off his brow.

Why was he even surprised by his odd reaction? Nothing made sense where Issy was concerned, for the simple reason that he stopped thinking altogether whenever she was around. He was probably lucky the sudden rush of blood from his head hadn't left him with permanent brain damage.

Gio brought his feet off the table and rested his elbows on his knees. He poured himself a glass of the iced water and gulped it down. Much more concerning was his idiot behaviour this afternoon.

He'd decided at an early age never to be controlled

by his lust or his emotions—yet he'd been controlled by both as soon as he'd spotted Issy downstairs.

But then, this wasn't the first time Issy had torpedoed his self-control.

Images swirled of Issy at seventeen, her eyes brimming with adulation, her beautiful body gilded by moonlight, the scent of fresh earth and young lust in the air.

She'd caught him in a moment of weakness ten years ago, but he still didn't understand why he'd given in to her innocent attempts to seduce him. The way things had ended had been messy and unnecessary—and he had to take the lion's share of the blame.

He rolled the chilled glass across his forehead. Damn Issy Helligan. At seventeen she had been irresistible. How could she be even more so now?

Standing, he crossed to the window and peered out at the tourists and office workers jostling for space on the pavement below.

Why was he even worrying about this? He would never see Issy again. He'd offered her money, and she'd declined. End of story.

But then his gaze caught on a familiar shock of red curls weaving through the crowd. With her raincoat barely covering her bottom, and those ludicrous boots riding halfway up her thighs, she stood out like a beacon.

As he studied her, striding away disguised as a high-class hooker, a picture formed of Issy ten years ago, with the vivid blue of her eyes shining with innocence and hope and a terminal case of hero-worship. He heard the echo of her voice, telling him she would love him forever.

And the jolt punched him in the chest again.

* * *

'Iss, I've got dreadful news.'

Issy glanced over as her admin assistant Maxi put down the phone, peering over the teetering pile of papers on her desk. Maxi's small pixie-like face had gone chalk white.

'What is it?' Issy asked, her heart sinking. Had one of the company broken a leg or something equally catastrophic? Maxi was exceptionally calm and steady. Panicking was Issy's forte.

Issy steeled herself for very bad news. But, really, how much worse could it get?

After her aborted singergram a week ago, the singing telegram business had dried up completely. The three grants they'd applied for had been awarded elsewhere, and all her sponsorship requests had come back negative. She'd spent the week frantically cold-calling a new list of potential but even less likely donors, while also arranging the schedule for a season of plays that would probably never go into production. And the boiler had sprung another leak. Not a problem in the height of summer, but come autumn it would be another major expenditure they couldn't afford. Assuming they still had a theatre to heat.

'That was the bank manager,' Maxi muttered.

Issy's heart sank to her toes. Okay, that was worse.

'He's demanding payment of the interest in ten working days. If we don't find the thirty thousand to cover the payments we've missed, he's calling in the bailiffs.'

'What the—?' Issy shouted.

Seeing Maxi flinch, she held on to the swear word

that wanted to fly out of her mouth and deafen the whole of Islington.

'That toerag,' she sneered. 'But we *paid* something. Not the full amount, I know, but something.' Her fingers clenched so tightly on her pen she felt as if she were fighting off rigor mortis. 'He can't do that.'

'Apparently he can,' Maxi replied, her voice despondent. 'Our last payment was so low it amounts to defaulting on the loan. Technically.' She huffed. 'Toerag is right.'

'Remind me not to send Mr Toerag any more complimentary tickets,' Issy replied, trying to put some of her usual spirit into the put-down. But her heart wasn't in it, her anger having deflated like a burst party balloon.

This wasn't the banker manager's fault. Not really. The theatre had been skirting the edge of a precipice for months; all he'd done was give it the final nudge into the abyss.

Issy crossed to the office's single dust-covered window and stared at the back alley below, which looked even grottier than usual this morning.

Maybe a broken leg wouldn't have been so bad. Three weeks laid up in bed on a morphine drip with excruciating pain shooting through her entire body couldn't make her feel any worse than she did at this moment.

She'd failed. Utterly and completely. How was she going to break the news to everyone? To Dave their principal director, to Terri and Steve and the rest of their regular crew of actors and technicians, not to mention all the ushers and front-of-house staff? They'd worked so hard over the years, many of them offering their time and talent for free, to make this place work, to make it a success.

They'd have to stop all the outreach projects too, with the local schools and the church youth group, and the pensioners' drop-in centre.

She pressed her teeth into her bottom lip to stop it trembling.

'Is this finally it, then?'

Issy turned at the murmured question to see a suspicious sheen in her assistant's eyes.

'Are we going to have to tell Dave and the troops?' Maxi asked carefully. 'They'll be devastated. They've worked so hard. We all have.'

'No. Not yet.' Issy scrubbed her hands down her face, forced the lump back down her throat.

Stop being such a wimp.

The Crown and Feathers Theatre wasn't going dark. Not on her watch. Not until the fat lady was singing. And until Issy Helligan admitted defeat the fat lady could keep her big mouth shut.

'Let's keep it quiet for a bit longer.' No point in telling anyone how bad things were until she absolutely had to. Which would be when the bailiffs arrived and started carting away crucial parts of the stage. 'There must be some avenue we haven't explored yet.'

Think, woman, think.

They had two whole weeks. There had to be something they could do.

'I can't think of any,' Maxi said. 'We've both been racking our brains for months over this. If there's an avenue we haven't tried, it's probably a dead end.' Maxi gave a hollow laugh. 'I even had a dream last night about us begging Prince Charles to become our patron.'

'What did he say?' Issy asked absently, eager to be distracted. Her head was starting to hurt.

'I woke up before he gave me an answer,' Maxi said dejectedly, giving a heartfelt sigh. 'If only we knew someone who was loaded and had a passion for the dramatic arts. All our problems would be over.'

Issy swallowed heavily, Maxi's words reminding her of someone she'd been trying extra hard to forget in the past seven days.

Not that. Anything but that.

She sat back down in her chair with an audible plop.

'What's the matter?' Maxi asked, sounding concerned. 'You've gone white as a sheet.'

'I do know someone. He's a duke.'

'A duke!' Maxi bounced up. 'You're friends with a duke, and we haven't approached him for sponsorship yet?' She waved the comment away as she rushed to Issy's desk, her eyes bright with newfound hope. 'Does he have a passion for theatre?'

'Not that I know of.' And they weren't exactly friends either.

Heat rose up her neck and her nipples pebbled painfully as the memory she'd been trying to suppress for a week burst back to life.

No, they definitely weren't friends.

'But he is loaded,' she added, not wanting to extinguish the excitement in Maxi's gaze.

Or she assumed Gio was loaded. She had absolutely no idea what he did for a living, or even if he did anything. But he was a duke. And he kept a room at the swanky gentlemen's club. And hadn't he said something about renovating Hamilton Hall? Surely it made sense to assume he must be loaded?

Issy crossed her arms over her chest as her breasts began to throb. Something they'd been doing on a regular basis for days, every time she thought about Gio and his hot, insistent lips… She shook her head. Those thoughts had been coming a lot thicker and faster than she wanted to admit. And not just those thoughts, but other ones—which involved his lips and tongue and teeth and hands on the whole of her naked body, driving her to untold…

Issy squeezed her pulsating breasts harder as all her nerve endings started to tingle.

'When are you going to see him again? Can you contact him today?'

She tensed at Maxi's eager question.

'What's wrong?' Maxi asked, the light leaving her eyes. 'You don't look all that enthusiastic.'

'It's a long shot, Max. At best.'

More than a long shot, if she were being totally honest. She'd told Gio she detested him, for goodness' sake. Like a spoilt child. And, while it had given her some satisfaction at the time, and she doubted he cared *what* she thought of him, it wasn't going to make begging him for money any easier.

Maxi cocked her head to one side, looking concerned. 'Exactly how well do you know this duke? Because you've gone bright red…'

'Well enough.' Maybe too well.

She needed a strategy before she saw Gio again. A foolproof strategy. If she was going to have any hope of winning a stay of execution for the theatre—and keeping even a small part of her dignity intact.

Issy felt as if she'd travelled back in time as she stepped off the train at the tiny Hampshire station of Hamilton's

Cross and walked down the platform. It was a journey she'd done dozens of times during her childhood and adolescence when her widowed mother Edie had been housekeeper at the Hall.

Seeing her reflection in the glass door of the ticket office—which never seemed to be open then and wasn't now—Issy congratulated herself on how much her appearance had changed from that dumpy schoolgirl with the fire-engine red hair. The chic emerald silk dress with matching pumps, accented with her favourite chunky necklace and designer sunglasses, looked a good deal more sophisticated than the ill-fitting school uniform, for starters. Teased into a waterfall of cork-screw curls instead of the unruly fuzzball of her childhood, even her vivid red hair now looked more Rita Hayworth than Little Orphan Annie.

The thought gave her a confidence boost as she headed for the newspaper booth which doubled as a mini-cab office. A boost she desperately needed after spending half the night struggling to figure out a workable strategy for her meeting with Gio.

If only she hadn't told him she detested him!

Unfortunately the strategy she'd settled on—to be businesslike and efficient and not lose her cool— seemed disappointingly vague and far from foolproof as zero hour approached.

She tucked the stray curls behind her ear and gripped the shoulder strap on her satchel-style briefcase. Full of paperwork about the theatre—including details of the loans, financial projections, the stunning reviews from their summer season and her plans for next season—the briefcase put the finishing touch on her smart, savvy career-woman act.

Not that it was an act, *per se*, she corrected. She *was* smart and savvy and a career woman—of sorts. Unfortunately she was also a nervous wreck—after a sleepless night spent contemplating all the things that could go wrong today.

Having discarded the idea of informing Gio of her visit beforehand—fairly certain he would refuse to see her—she had surprise on her side. But from what she'd learned about Gio after scouring the internet for information, surprise was about all she had.

The startling revelation that Gio was now a world-renowned architect, with a reputation for striking and innovative designs and a practice which was one of the most sought-after in Europe, hadn't helped with her nervous breakdown one bit.

Okay, Gio was definitely rich. That had to be a plus, given the reason why she was here. But the discovery that the wild, reckless boy she had idolised had made such a staggering success of his life had brought with it a strange poignancy which didn't bode well for their meeting.

And that was without factoring in the way her body had responded to him a week ago. Which, try as she might, she still hadn't been able to forget.

She was here for one reason and one reason only, and she was not going to lose sight of that fact. No matter what. Or the theatre's last hope would be dashed for good.

She had to stick to her plan. She would promote the theatre and do her absolute utmost to persuade Gio that investing in a sponsorship would give his company added profile in the British marketplace. If all else failed she'd remind him that he had offered her financial help. But under no circumstances would she let their history—or her hormones—sway her from her goal. No matter what the provocation—or the temptation.

'Good Lord, is that you, Issy Helligan? Haven't you grown up!'

Issy beamed a smile at the short, balding man sitting in the mini-cab cubicle. 'Frank, you're still here!' she said, delighted to see a familiar face.

'That I am,' the elderly man said bashfully, as his bald patch went a mottled red. 'How's your mother these days? Still living in Cornwall?'

'That's right, she loves it there,' Issy replied, grateful for the distraction.

'Awful shame about the Duke's passing last summer,' Frank continued, his smile dying. 'Son's back you know. Doing up the Hall. Although he never saw fit to come to the funeral. 'Spect your mother told you that?'

Edie hadn't, because her mother knew better than to talk to her about Gio after that fateful summer.

But the news that Gio hadn't bothered to attend his own father's funeral didn't surprise Issy. He and his father had always had a miserably dysfunctional relationship, evidenced by the heated arguments and chilly silences she and her mother had witnessed during the summers Gio spent at the Hall.

She'd once romanticised Gio's troubled teenage years, casting him as a misunderstood bad boy, torn between two parents who hated each other's guts and used their only child as a battering ram. She'd stopped romanticising Gio's behaviour a decade ago. And she had no desire to remember that surly, unhappy boy now.

It might make her underestimate the man he had become.

'Actually, I don't suppose you know whether Gio's at the Hall today? I came to pay him a visit.'

According to the articles she'd read, Gio lived in Italy, but his office in Florence had told her he was in England. So she'd taken a chance he might be at the Hall.

'Oh, aye—yes, he's here,' said Frank, making Issy's pulse skitter. 'Came in yesterday evening by helicopter, no less—or so Milly at the post office says. I took the council planners over to the Hall for a meeting an hour ago.'

'Could I get a lift too?' she said quickly, before she lost her nerve.

Frank grinned and grabbed his car keys. 'That's what I'm here for.'

He bolted the booth and directed her to the battered taxi-cab parked out front.

'I'll put your journey out on the house, for old times' sake,' he said cheerfully as he opened the door.

Issy tensed as she settled in the back seat.

No way was she going to think about old times. Especially her old times with Gio.

She snapped the seat belt on, determined to wipe every last one of those memories from her consciousness.

But as the car accelerated away from the kerb, and the familiar hedgerows and grass verges sped past on the twenty-minute drive to the Hall, the old times came flooding back regardless.

CHAPTER THREE

Ten Years Earlier

'I CAN'T believe you're really going to do it tonight. What if your mum finds out?'

'Shh, Melly,' Issy hissed as she craned her neck to check on the younger girls sitting at the front of the school bus. 'Keep your voice down.'

As upper sixth-formers, they had the coveted back seat all to themselves, but she didn't want anyone over-hearing the conversation. Especially as she didn't even want to be *having* this conversation.

When she'd told her best friend about her secret plan to loose her virginity to Giovanni Hamilton two years before, it had been thrilling and exciting. A forbidden topic they could discuss for hours on the long, boring bus ride home every day. And it had had about as much chance of actually happening as Melanie's equally thrilling and exciting and endlessly discussed plan to lose her virginity to Gary Barlow from *Take That*.

Gio had been completely unattainable back then. When she'd been fifteen and he'd been nineteen the four years between them had seemed like an eternity.

But it hadn't always been that way.

When Issy and her mother had first come to live at the Hall, and Gio had appeared that first summer, the two of them had become fast friends and partners in crime. To a nine-year-old tomboy who was used to spending hours on her own in the Hall's grounds, Gio had been a godsend. A moody, intense thirteen-year-old boy with brown eyes so beautiful they'd made her heart skip, a fascinating command of swear words in both English and Italian, and a quick, creative mind with a talent for thinking up forbidden adventures, Gio had been more captivating than a character from one of Issy's adventure books.

Best of all, Gio had needed her as much as she'd needed him. Issy had seen the sadness in his eyes when his father shouted at him—which seemed to be all the time—and it had made her stomach hurt. But she'd discovered that if she chatted to him, if she made him laugh, she could take the sad look away.

At fifteen, though, when she'd first formulated her plan to lose her virginity to him, her childhood friendship with Gio had slipped into awkward adolescent yearning.

She'd been gawky and spotty, with a figure her mum had insisted on calling 'womanly' but Issy thought was just plain fat, while Gio had been tall, tanned and gorgeous. A modern-day Heathcliff, with the looks of a Roman god and a wildness about him that drew every female within a twenty-mile radius like a magnet.

At nineteen, Gio already had a formidable reputation with women. And one night that summer Issy had seen the evidence for herself.

Creeping down to get a glass of water, she'd heard

moaning coming from the darkened dining room. Getting as close as she could without being spotted, she had watched, transfixed, as Gio's lean, fully-clothed body towered over a mostly naked woman lying on her back on the Duke's oak table. It had taken Issy a moment to recognise the writhing female as Maya Carrington, a thirty-something divorcée who had arrived for the Duke's weekend house party that afternoon.

Issy hadn't been able to look away as Gio's long, tanned fingers unclipped the front hook of Maya's black lace push-up bra, then moulded her full breasts. Issy had blushed to the roots of her hair at the socialite's soft sobs as Gio traced a line with his tongue over her prominent nipples, then nipped at them with his teeth as his hand disappeared between Maya's thighs.

Issy had dashed back to bed, her glass of water sloshing all over the stairs with her palm pressed against her pyjama bottoms to ease the brutal ache between her legs as her ragged breathing made her heart race.

She'd dreamt about Gio doing the same thing to her that night and for many nights afterwards, always waking up soaked in sweat, her breasts heavy and tender to the touch, her nipples rigid and that same cruel ache between her legs.

But Gio had never stopped treating her like a child. During that last visit two years ago, when he'd paid so much attention to Maya, he'd barely even spoken to her.

Then, the day before, something magical had happened.

He'd appeared at the school gates on his motorbike, looking surly and tense, and told her the school bus had been cancelled and her mother had asked him to give her a lift home. She hadn't seen Gio in two long years, and the feel of his muscled back pressing into her budding breasts had sent her senses into a blur of rioting hormones. She'd spent today reliving the experience in minute detail for her starstruck classmates, but in reality she'd had to make most of it up, because she'd been so excited she could barely remember a thing.

And then this morning she'd caught him looking at her while he was having breakfast with her and her mother, and just for a second she'd seen the same awareness in those turbulent brown eyes that she had always had in her heart.

She didn't have a schoolgirl crush on Gio. She loved him. Deeply and completely. And not just because of his exotic male beauty and the fact that all the other girls fancied him too. But because she knew things about him that no one else knew. Unfortunately, her attempts to flirt with him that morning had been ignored.

It was past time to take matters into her own hands.

What if Gio didn't come back again for another two years? She'd be an old woman of nineteen by then, and he might have got married or something. Tonight she would make him notice her. She would go to his room and get him to do what he'd been doing to Maya Carrington two years ago. Except this time it would be a thousand times more special, because she loved him and Maya hadn't.

But the last thing she'd wanted to do was discuss her plans with Melanie. It made Issy feel sneaky and juvenile and dishonest. As if she was tricking Gio. When she really wasn't. She should never have mentioned the motorcycle ride. Because Melly had latched on to the information, put two and two together and unfortunately made four. And now she wouldn't let the topic drop.

'What will your mum say?' Melanie asked in a stage whisper.

'Nothing. She's not going to find out,' she whispered back, pushing aside the little spurt of guilt.

Up till now she'd told her mother everything. Because it had been just the two of them for so long Edie had been a confidante and a friend, as well as her mum. But when Issy had tried to bring up the subject of Gio as casually as possible after breakfast her mother had been surprisingly stern with her.

'Don't hassle him. He has more than enough to deal with,' Edie had said cryptically while she pounded dough. 'I saw you flirting with him. And, while I understand the lure of someone as dashing and dangerous as Gio Hamilton, I don't want to see you get hurt when he turns you down.'

The comment had made Issy feel as if she were ten years old again—sheltered and patronised and excluded from all the conversations that mattered—and still trailing after Gio like a lovesick puppy dog.

What did Gio have to deal with? Why wouldn't anyone tell her? And what made her mum so sure he would turn her down? She wanted to help him. To be *there* for him. And she wanted to know what it felt like to be kissed by a man who knew how, instead of the awkward boys she'd kissed before.

But everyone treated her as if she was too young and didn't know her own mind. When she wasn't. And she did.

She'd wanted to tell her mum that, but had decided not to. Edie had looked so troubled when they'd both heard the shouting match between Gio and his father the night before, coming through the air vent from the library.

'Do you have protection?' Melanie continued, still talking in the stupid stage whisper.

'Yes.' She'd bought the condoms months ago, just in case Gio visited this summer, and had gone all the way to Middleton to get them, so Mrs Green the pharmacist in Hamilton's Cross wouldn't tell her mum.

'Aren't you worried that it'll hurt? Jenny Merrin said it hurt like mad when she did it with Johnny Baxter, and I bet Gio's…' Melanie paused for effect. 'You know…is twice the size. Look how tall he is.'

'No, of course not,' she said, starting to get annoyed.

Yes, it would probably hurt a bit, she knew that, but she wasn't a coward. And if you loved someone you didn't worry about how big their 'you know what' was. She'd read in *Cosmo* only last week that size didn't matter.

The bus took the turning into the Hall's drive and she breathed a sigh of relief. She wanted to get home. There was so much to do before dinnertime. She needed to have a bath and wash her hair, wax her legs, do her nails, try on the three different outfits she had shortlisted for tonight one last time. This was going to be the most important night of her life, and she wanted to look the part. To prove to Gio she wasn't a babyish tomboy any more, or a gawky, overweight teenager.

She felt the now constant ache between her legs and the tight ball of emotion in her throat and knew she was doing the right thing.

As the bus driver braked, she leapt up. But Melanie grabbed her wrist.

'I'm so jealous of you,' Melanie said, her eyes

shining with sincerity. 'He's so dishy. I hope it doesn't hurt too much.'

'It won't,' Issy said.

Gio wouldn't hurt her—not intentionally—of that much she was certain.

So much had changed in the last few years, but not that. Before she'd fallen in love with him he'd been like a big brother to her. Teasing her and letting her follow him around. Listening to her talk about the father she barely remembered and telling her she shouldn't care if she didn't have a dad. That fathers were a pain any way. Things had been difficult, tense between her and Gio since she'd grown up—partly because they weren't little kids anymore, but mostly because he'd become so distant.

His relationship with his father had got so bad he hardly ever came to visit the Hall any more, and when she did see him now his brooding intensity had become like a shield, demanding that everyone—even her—keep out.

But tonight she would be able to get him back again. That moody, magnetic boy would be her friend again, but more than that he'd be her lover, and he'd know he could tell her anything. And everything would be wonderful.

Issy crept through the darkness. Feeling her way past the kitchen garden wall, she pushed the gate into the orchard. And eased out the breath she'd been holding when the hinge barely creaked. She sucked in air scented with ripe apples and the faint tinge of tobacco.

Kicking off her shoes, she stepped off the path onto the dewy grass. It would ruin the effect slightly, but she didn't want to trip over a root in her heels. After waiting for nearly three hours for Gio to come home she was nervous enough already, falling on her face would not be the way to go.

She pressed the flat of her hand to her stomach and felt the butterfly flutter of panic and excitement. Squinting into the shadows, she saw the red glow of a cigarette tip and her heart punched her ribcage. He'd always come to the orchard before whenever he argued with his father. She'd known he would be here.

'Gio?' she called softly, tiptoeing towards the silent shape hidden beneath a tree burdened with summer fruit.

The red glow disappeared as he stamped the cigarette out.

'What do you want?' He sounded edgy, dismissive. She ignored the tightening in her chest. He was upset. He didn't mean to be cruel.

She didn't know what his father and he had been shouting about this time, but she knew it had been bad—worse than the night before.

'Is everything all right? I heard you and the Duke—'

'Great,' he interrupted. 'Everything's great. Now, go away.'

As she stepped beneath the canopy of leaves her eyes adjusted to the lack of light and she could make out his features. The chiselled cheekbones shadowed with stubble, the dark brows, the strong chin and jawline. He stood with his back propped against the tree trunk, his arms crossed and his head bent. The pose might have been casual but for the tension that crackled in the air around him.

'No, I won't go away,' she said, surprised by the forcefulness in her voice. 'Everything's not great.'

His head lifted and the hairs on her nape prickled.

She could feel his eyes on her, even though she couldn't make out his expression, could smell his distinctive male scent, that heady mix of soap and musk.

'I mean it, Iss,' he said, the low tone brittle. 'Go away. I'm not in the mood.'

She stepped closer, feeling as if she were encroaching on a wild animal. 'I'm not going anywhere,' she said, her voice trembling but determined. 'What did he say, Gio? Why are you so upset?'

She placed a palm on his cheek, and he jerked back.

'Don't touch me.' The words were rough, but beneath it she could hear panic.

'Why not? I want to touch you.'

'Yeah?' The snarl was wild, uncontrolled. But before she could register the shock he grabbed a fistful of the silk at her waist and hauled her against him.

Her breath gushed out, adrenaline coursing through her body as he held her hips. She could feel every inch of him. The thick ridge of something rubbed against the juncture of her thighs, and she squirmed instinctively.

He swore. Then his mouth crushed hers. The faint taste of tobacco made all the more intoxicating by heat and demand.

He cradled her head, held her steady as his tongue plunged. She gasped, her fingers fisting in the soft cotton of his T-shirt as she clung on. She opened her mouth wider, surrendered to a rush of arousal so new, so thrilling, it made her head spin.

He lurched back, held her at arm's length. 'What the hell are you doing?'

'Kissing you back,' she said, confused by the accusatory tone.

Why had he stopped? When it had felt so good?

'Well, don't,' he said, his voice sharp. His fingers released her and he crossed his arms back over his chest.

'Why not?' she cried. She wanted him to carry on kissing her, to keep kissing her forever.

'Issy, go away.' The anger sounded almost weary now. 'You don't know what you're doing. I'm not some kid you can practise your kissing technique on. And I don't take little girls to bed.'

'I'm not a little girl. I'm a woman, with a woman's desires,' she added, hoping the line she'd read in one of her romance novels didn't sound too cheesy.

'Yeah, right.' Her confidence deflated at the doubtful tone. 'How old *are* you?'

'I'm nearly eighteen,' she said with bravado. Or rather she would be in six months' time. 'And I do know what I'm doing.' Or at least she was trying her best to know. Surely he could teach her the rest?

The silence seemed to spread out between them, the only noise the pummelling of her own heartbeat and the hushed sound of their breathing.

He reached out and traced his thumb down her cheek. 'For God's sake, Issy, don't tempt me,' he murmured. 'Not unless you're sure.'

'I am sure. I have been for a long time,' she replied. He needed her. She hadn't imagined it. The thought was so thrilling she locked her knees to stay upright.

He cradled her cheek. She leant into his palm.

'I want you, Gio,' she whispered, covering his hand with hers. 'Don't you want me?'

It was the hardest question she'd ever had to ask. If he said no now she would be devastated. She caught her breath and held it.

He pushed his fingers into her hair, rubbed his thumb against the strands. 'Yeah, I want you, Isadora. Too damn much.'

Her breath released in a rush as he pulled her close and his lips slanted across hers. The kiss was sensual, seeking this time, his tongue tracing the contours of her mouth with a tenderness and care that had her shuddering.

He leaned back. 'Are you sure you know what you're doing?' he said, searching her face, his hands framing her cheeks. 'I don't want to hurt you.'

'You won't hurt me. You couldn't.'

Dropping his hands, he linked his fingers through hers. 'Let's take this inside.'

Nervous anticipation made her stumble as he led her through the moonlit gardens and the gloomy shadows of the house's back staircase, his strides long and assured and full of purpose. She took the stairs two at a time, the first tremors of doubt making her legs shake. When he shoved open the door to his room on the second floor her heart beat so hard she was convinced he would hear it too.

He reached to switch on the light and she grasped his wrist.

'Could you leave the light off?' she blurted. She let go of his arm, desperate to disguise the quiver in her voice.

'Why?' he asked.

She scoured her mind for a viable excuse. If he knew how inexperienced she was he might stop, and she couldn't bear that. 'It's…it's more romantic,' she said.

He seemed to study her in the darkness for an eternity before he crossed the room and opened the drapes, letting the moonlight flood in.

'Issy, I don't do permanent,' he said as he came back to her. He brushed a kiss on her forehead. 'You know that, right?'

She nodded, not trusting herself to speak. That would change, she was sure of it, once he had the proof of how much she loved him. She draped her arms over his shoulders, calling on every ounce of her fledgling skills as an actress. She'd told him she wasn't a little girl. It was time to stop behaving like one.

'Yes, I know.' Driving her fingers into the short hair at his nape, she took a deep breath of his scent, revelled in the feel of him as he pressed her back against the door, captured her waist in hot palms.

'Good,' he muttered, as his teeth bit into her earlobe.

She shuddered, letting the delicious shiver race down her spine as his lips feasted on the pulse-point in her neck. The hot, vicious ache at her core throbbed in time with her deafening heartbeat. She reminded herself to breathe as he drew the zipper on her dress down, tugged her arms free. The shimmering silk puddled at her feet. She clung to his neck, the heady thrill making her dizzy as he bent and lifted her easily into his arms.

This was really happening at last. After years of fantasising, her dreams were coming true.

Silvery light gilded his chest as he cast off his T-shirt. He unfastened his belt and she looked away, suddenly overwhelmed. He looked so powerful, so strong, so completely male. The mattress dipped as he joined her on the bed. His hand settled on her midriff, drew her towards him. She felt the heat of his big body, the thick outline prodding her thigh.

His face looked hard, intent in the shadows, as his deft fingers freed her breasts from the confining lace of her bra.

'You're beautiful, Issy' he said, his voice low and strained as one rough fingertip traced over her nipple. 'I want to look at you properly. Let's turn on the light.'

She shook her head, mute with longing and panic. 'Please—I like it dark,' she said, hoping she sounded as if she knew what she was talking about.

'Okay,' he said. 'But next time we do it my way.' Her heart soared at the mention of *next time*, and then he bent his head and captured the pebble-hard nipple in his teeth.

A sob escaped as sensation raw and hot arrowed down to her core. She arched up, bucked under him as he suckled. Damp heat gushed between her thighs.

Her hands fisted in the sheets as she tried to cling to sanity. Tried to stop herself from shattering into a billion pieces.

'Open your legs for me, *bella*.' The urgent whisper penetrated, and her knees relaxed to let his palm cup her core.

Strong fingers probed, stroked, caressed, touching and then retreating. She cried out, begged, until he stayed right at the centre of ecstasy. The wave rose with shocking speed, and then slammed into her with the force and fury of a tsunami.

She struggled to find focus, to claw her way back to consciousness as hot hands held her hips. He loomed above her in the darkness. 'Dammit, Issy, I can't wait. Is that okay?'

She couldn't register his meaning, but nodded as he

fumbled with something in the darkness. Then she felt it—huge, unyielding but soft as velvet, spearing through her swollen flesh. A heavy thrust brought sharp, rending pain. She strained beneath him, a choking sob lodged in her throat.

He stopped, tried to draw out. 'Issy, what the—?'

'Please, don't stop.' She gasped the plea, gripping shoulders tight with bunched muscle. 'It doesn't hurt.' And it didn't. Not any more. The overwhelming pressure, the stretched feeling, had become a pulsing ache, clamouring for release.

He swore, but pressed back in slowly, carefully. Her hands slipped on slick skin, hard sinew, her jagged breathing matching the relentless thrusts. She heard his harsh grunts, her own sobs of release as the tsunami built to another bold crescendo, threatening so much more than before. Her scream of release echoed in her head as the final wave crashed, exploding through her as she hurtled over the top.

'For God's sake, Issy. You were a bloody virgin.'

Her eyelids fluttered open—and the bedside light snapped on, blinding her.

'I know.' She threw her arm up to cover her eyes, registering his temper. What had she done?

Tremors racked her body as afterglow turned neatly to aftershock.

'Shh. Calm down.' The hammer-beats of his heart thudded against her ear as he settled her head on his chest, gathered her close. 'I'm sorry, Iss. Stop shaking.' He brushed the locks from her brow. 'Are you okay? Did I hurt you?'

She opened her eyes. The soft light illuminated his features clearly. Love swept through her, more intense, more real than ever before as she saw the worry, the concern.

A smile spread as euphoria leaped in her chest. 'Yes, I'm okay.' She snuggled into his embrace and sighed. Despite the soreness between her legs, she'd never felt more complete, more wonderful in her life. 'I never dreamed it could be that amazing.'

He shifted back. Holding her chin, he lifted her face. 'Wait a minute. I asked you.' His eyes narrowed. 'Why didn't you tell me the truth?'

'I don't…I don't understand,' she stammered, chilling as he took his arm from around her and sat up.

Whipping back the sheet, he turned his back to her and stood up. As he paced across the room, the sight of his naked body had the heat between her thighs sizzling back to life. But then she noticed the sharp, irritated movements as he yanked on his jeans, pulled on the T-shirt.

'Is something wrong?' she asked, her pulse stuttering. She clasped the sheet to her chest. This wasn't right. This wasn't how it was supposed to be. This was the moment when they were supposed to declare their undying love for each other.

He twisted round, sent her a look that had colour rising in her cheeks.

'I asked you if you were a virgin.' The harsh tone made her flinch. 'Why did you lie?'

'I…' Had he asked? She gave her head a quick shake. 'I don't…I didn't mean to lie.'

'Sure you did.' He flung the words over his shoulder as he grabbed a bag from the closet, swept the few personal items on top of the dresser into it. He ripped open the top drawer, scooped out his clothes, shoved them in too. The tense movements radiated controlled anger.

Tears stung her eyes, swelled in her throat. 'Please, Gio, I don't understand. What are you doing?'

'I'm leaving. What does it look like?' He slashed the zipper closed.

Facing her at last, he slung the holdall over his shoulder. 'I'm sorry if I hurt you. I should have stopped once I realised what was going on. But I couldn't. And that's on me. But whatever game you were playing, it's over now.'

'It's not a game.' She clung to the sheet, kneeled on the mattress, desperate to hold on to her dream. This was a silly misunderstanding. He loved her. He needed her. She needed him. Hadn't they proved that together?

'I love you Gio. I've always loved you. I always will. We were meant to be together.'

He went completely still, and then his eyebrow rose in cynical enquiry. 'Are you nuts? Grow up, for heaven's sake.'

The cruel words made her shrink inside herself. She sank back, her body quaking as she watched him stamp on his boots and walk to the door.

He couldn't be leaving. Not now, not like this, not after everything they'd just done.

'Don't go, Gio. You have to stay.'

He turned, his hand on the door handle. She braced herself for another shot. But instead of anger she saw regret.

'There's nothing for me here.' His voice sounded

hollow, but the bitterness in the words still made the agonising pain a thousands times worse. 'There never was.'

A single jerking sob caught in her throat and the tears streamed down her cheeks.

'Don't cry, Issy. Believe me, it's not worth it. When you figure that out, you'll thank me for this.'

CHAPTER FOUR

The Present

Issy released her fingers to ease their death grip on the handle of her briefcase.

How could every damn detail of that night still be so vivid?

Not just the anguish and the pain, but the euphoria and the hope too—even the intense pleasure of their lovemaking. How many times had she played it over in her head in the months and years that had followed? Hundreds? Thousands?

Way too many times, that was for sure.

She forced herself to ignore the pressure in her chest at the thought of Gio's parting words that night. They couldn't hurt her. Not any more. All her tears had dried up a long time ago.

Gio had been right about one thing. She should thank him. He'd taught her an important lesson. Never open your heart to someone until you're positive they're the prince and not the frog. And don't be fooled by fancy packaging.

'Nearly there,' Frank called cheerfully from the front

seat. 'Wait till you see what the lad's done with the place. Amazing, it is. Must have cost a fortune by my reckoning.'

Issy drew a deep breath, eased it out through her teeth. No more ancient history. She had enough of a mountain to climb just concentrating on the here and now.

She glanced out of the window. Only to have her fingers tighten on the briefcase again.

Amazing wasn't the word. More like awe-inspiring, Issy thought as she stepped out of the cab onto the newly pebbled driveway and gaped at the magnificent Georgian frontage of her former home. Gio hadn't just restored the Hall, he'd improved upon it. The place looked magnificent. The bright sand-blasted stone gleamed in the sunshine. The columns at the front of the house had always looked forbidding to her as a child, but a terrace had been added which gave the house a welcoming Mediterranean feel.

Having failed to persuade Frank to take a fare for the journey, she bade him goodbye.

As the cab pulled away, she gazed up at the Hall. Why did Gio's transformation of the place make her feel even more daunted?

She adjusted the strap of her briefcase and slung it over her shoulder.

Don't be silly. Remember, this isn't about you, or Gio, or the Hall. It's about the theatre—and shutting the fat lady up long enough to see out another season. Absolutely no more trips down memory lane allowed. The past is dead, and it needs to stay that way.

'Hey, can I help you?'

She glanced round to see a young man strolling towards her. Her fingers locked on the strap.

Curtain up.

'Hi, my name's Isadora Helligan.' She thrust out her hand as he approached. 'I'm here to see Giovanni Hamilton.'

Stopping in front of her, he ran his fingers through his sandy-blond hair and sent her a quizzical smile. 'Hi, Jack Bradshaw.' He took her hand and gave it a hearty shake. 'I'm Gio's PA.' He put his hand back in his pocket. 'I'm sorry, I keep Gio's diary, but…' He paused, looking a little perplexed. 'Do you have an appointment?'

Not quite.

'Yes,' she lied smoothly. 'Gio made it himself a week ago. He must have forgotten to tell you.'

If Gio was going to kick her out, he would have to do it personally.

'No problem,' Jack replied. 'It won't be the first time. Creative geniuses rarely pay attention to the little details.' He extended his arm towards the Hall. 'He's finishing up with the planners on the pool terrace. Why don't you come through?'

As Jack led the way, Issy found herself too busy gazing at all the changes Gio had made to get any more nervous thinking about what she had to do.

How had he managed to get so much light into the interior of the building? And how come the place looked so spacious and open whereas before it had always seemed poky and austere?

The nerves kicked back in, though, as she stepped out onto the pool terrace and saw Gio. Tall and gorgeous and effortlessly commanding in grey linen trousers and an

open-necked shirt, he stood on the other side of the
empty pool, chatting with a couple of men in ill-fitting
suits who were several inches shorter than him. Almost
as if he sensed her standing there, staring at him, he
turned his head. She could have sworn she felt the heat
of his gaze as it raked over her figure.

Her stomach tensed as an answering heat bloomed
in her cheeks.

She watched as he shook hands with the two men and
then walked towards her over the newly mown grass.
And was immediately thrown back in time to all the
times she'd watched him in the past.

She'd always adored the way Gio moved, with that
relaxed, languid, confident stride, as if he was completely comfortable in his own skin. He'd always been
the sort of man to turn heads, even as a teenager, but age
had added an air of dominance to that dangerous sex
appeal. Unfortunately, the full package was even more
devastating now. Tanned Mediterranean skin, the mus-
cular, broad-shouldered physique and slim hips, that
sharply handsome face and his rich chestnut-brown hair
which had once been long enough to tie in a ponytail—
to annoy his father she suspected—but was now cut
short and fell in careless waves across his brow.

Was it any surprise she'd idolised him once—and
mistaken him for the prince? Thank God she didn't
idolise him any more. Unfortunately, the assertion
didn't seem to be doing a thing for the heat cascading
through her as he took his own sweet time strolling
towards her.

Her heartbeat spiked, her nerve endings tingled and
adrenaline pumped through her veins. She fidgeted

with the bag's strap, trying to bring her breathing back under control.

Good grief, what on earth was happening to her? Had the extreme stress of the last few months turned her into a nymphomaniac?

Her knees wobbled ever so slightly as he drew level, a sensual, knowing smile tilting his lips.

'This is a surprise, Isadora,' he said, pronouncing her full name with the tiniest hint of Italy. 'You're looking a lot more…' His gaze flicked down her frame. Her knees wobbled some more. 'Sophisticated today.'

'Hello, Gio,' she said, being as businesslike as she could with her nipples thrusting against the front of her blouse like bullets.

Trust Gio to remind her of their last meeting. No way was he going to make this easy for her. But then she hadn't expected easy.

'I'm sorry to arrive unannounced,' she said, looking as meek as she could possibly manage. 'But I have something important I wanted to discuss with you.'

His gaze drifted to her chest. 'Really?'

She crossed her arms over her chest to cover her inappropriate reaction. Why hadn't she worn a padded bra? 'Yes, really,' she said, a little too curtly. 'Do you mind if we discuss it in private?'

If he was going to humiliate her, she'd rather not have an audience. Several of his employees were already staring at them from the other side of the pool.

'There are workmen all over the house,' he said calmly, but the challenge in his eyes was unmistakable as they fixed on her face. 'The only place we'll be able to have any privacy is in my bedroom.'

What? No way.

Her mind lurched back as the memories she'd been busy suppressing shot her blood pressure straight into the danger zone. But then she noticed the cynical curve of his lips and knew it wasn't a genuine invitation. He expected her to decline. Because he thought she couldn't handle the past, couldn't handle him.

Think again, Buster.

'That'd be great,' she said, even though her throat was now drier than the Gobi Desert. 'If you're sure you don't mind?' she added with a hint of defiance.

'Not at all,' he replied, not sounding as surprised as she'd hoped. He lifted his arm. 'I believe you know the way,' he said, every inch the amenable, impersonal host.

Blast him.

They climbed the back staircase without a word. His silent, indomitable presence starting to rattle her. How could he be so relaxed, so unmoved?

She cut the thought off. Of course he could be. What had happened in his bedroom all those years ago had never meant a thing to him. She pushed the residual flicker of hurt away, clinging to being businesslike and efficient. If he could be, so could she.

But even as the rallying cry sounded in her head he opened his bedroom door, and she had to brace herself against the painful memories. She caught his scent, that dizzying combination of soap and man, more potent this time without the masking hint of tobacco, as he held the door for her to walk in ahead of him.

Colour flooded up her neck as she stepped into the room where he had once stolen her innocence. And destroyed her dreams.

The walls were painted utilitarian white now, the bed a brand-new teak frame draped with pale blue linen, but the memories were all still there, as vivid and disturbing as yesterday. She could see herself kneeling on the bed, the sheet clutched to her chest, her heart shattering.

'So what exactly is it that's so important?'

She whirled round to see him leaning against the door, his arms folded over his chest, his expression indifferent. She held the briefcase in front of her, tried to control the rush of emotions. He was goading her deliberately. She had no idea why, but she wasn't going to let it mean anything.

'You offered me money. A week ago.'

His brows arrowed up. Seemed she'd surprised him at last.

'I wanted to know if the offer's still open,' she added.

'You came here to ask me for money?'

She heard the brittle edge and took a perverse pleasure in it. Good to know she could rattle him too.

'That's correct.'

'Well, now,' he said, pushing away from the door and strolling towards her. 'So what happened to the woman who has principles and wouldn't dare lower herself to take anything from me?'

He stopped in front of her, standing so close she could feel the heat of his body.

'It *was* you who said that? Wasn't it?'

'I apologise for that.' She lifted her chin to meet his gaze, refusing to take a step back. She knew perfectly well he was trying to intimidate her. She should never have said those stupid things, but he had provoked her. 'But I didn't think you cared what I thought,' she finished, knowing perfectly well her comments hadn't bothered him in the slightest.

He ran a finger down her cheek and she stiffened, shocking desire coiling in her gut at the unexpected touch.

'You'd be surprised what I care about,' he murmured.

She stepped back. Forced into retreat after all. How was he still able to fan the flames so easily?

'I should go,' she said hastily, her courage suddenly deserting her.

What on earth had possessed her to come here? He would never give her the money. All she'd done was humiliate herself for no reason.

But as she tried to step around him and make a dash for the door he grasped her upper arm.

'So it wasn't *that* important?' he said, a challenging glint in his eyes.

Spurred on by desperation and an unreasonable panic, her temper snapped. She yanked her arm out of his grasp. This wasn't a game. Not to her anyway. 'It *was* important. Not that you'd ever understand.'

She'd always been willing to fight for what she believed in. He'd never once done that. Because he'd never believed in anything.

He laughed, the sound harsh. 'Why don't you show me, then?' Holding both her arms, he hauled her closer. 'If you want the money so much, what do I get in return?'

'What do you want?' She hurled the words at him, angry, upset, and—God help her—desperately turned on.

His fingers flexed on her arms. 'You know what I want.' His jaw tightened. 'And you want it too. Except you always had to sugar-coat it with all that nonsense about love.'

The barb hit home, but did nothing to quell the flames licking at her core.

'Sex?' She huffed out a contemptuous laugh. Not easy when she was about to spontaneously combust. 'Is that all?' She pressed closer, rubbed provocatively against the thick ridge in his trousers. Past caring about pride, or maturity, or scruples, as temper and desire raged out of control.

He thought she was still the fanciful naïve virgin who expected love and commitment. Well, she wasn't, and she could prove it.

'If that's all you want, why don't you take it?' she goaded, revelling in the rush of power as his eyes darkened. 'You don't have to worry. I won't sugar-coat it a second time.'

His lips crushed hers. He tasted of fury and frustration and demand, his fingers caressing her scalp as he invaded her mouth. She clutched his shoulders and kissed him back, all thoughts of revenge, of vindication, incinerated by the firestorm of need.

He broke away first, only to swing her up in his arms. She fell back on the bed, feeling as if she were careering over Niagara Falls in a barrel—terrified and exhilarated, her body battered by its own sensual overload. He struggled to get the dress over her head, the sibilant hiss of rending fabric drowned out by their laboured breathing. She grasped his shirt, popping buttons, reached for the firm silky flesh beneath as he grappled with her bra, exposing her breasts.

He pushed her back on the pillows, kneeled over her. Unlike that first night, when she'd hidden herself from his sight, she basked in the intoxicating rush of desire as her nipples swelled and hardened under his assessing gaze.

He cupped the heavy orbs, rubbed his thumb over the engorged peaks.

'Dammit, you're even more beautiful than I remember.'

The stunned words touched her somewhere deep inside, but the fanciful emotion was lost as he bent forward and captured a nipple with his teeth. A staggered moan escaped as fire blazed down to her core. Grasping his cheeks, she pushed into his mouth. The rasp of stubble against her soft palms as primal as the crude heat burning at her centre.

She watched spellbound and desperate as he scrambled out of his own clothes. Kicking off his loafers, he wrestled out of the torn shirt, and dropped trousers and briefs in a crumpled heap to the floor.

Where once she'd been afraid to look at him, this time she devoured the dark male beauty of his body. Tanned skin, muscled shoulders, a lean ridged abdomen and powerful flanks all vied for her attention. But then her gaze fixed on the long, thick erection, and the tantalising bead of moisture at its tip. Her breath clogged in her lungs as he climbed onto the bed, caging her in.

Reaching, she closed her fingers around the hard, pulsing flesh. Vicious desire coiled as the magnificent erection leapt in response.

He pulled out of her grasp, deft fingers probing beneath the lace of her panties and finding the slick furnace at her core. Sensation assaulted her as he toyed with the hard nub. She sobbed, hurtling towards that brutal edge, but he withdrew.

Her eyes flew open, her senses straining. 'Don't stop!' she cried.

He laughed, the sound raw, and dragged off the thin swatch of lace, casting it over his shoulder. Leaning forward, he whispered against her ear. 'I'm going to be deep inside you when you come.'

She wanted to make a pithy comeback, but she could barely think let alone speak. All thoughts of caution, of consequences, were lost in the frantic hammer of her heartbeat as he grabbed a foil package from the bedside dresser and rolled on a condom.

He stroked her thighs, held her hips wide. Staring into her eyes, he gripped her bottom and pressed within. She gasped, quivered, stretched unbearably as he eased in up to the hilt.

He was a big man, and the fullness was as overwhelming and shocking now as it had been a decade ago. But this time she didn't panic. She held on, angling her hips as the pleasure intensified, battering her senses as he paused, allowing her to adjust to the brutal penetration.

She tensed, panting, her skin glowing with sweat as he began to move. She tried to hold back, to make it last, her body buffeted by rolling waves of ecstasy, but the rhythmic thrusts drove her towards orgasm at breakneck speed.

'Stay with me, *bella*,' he grunted, the molten chocolate of his eyes locking hot on her face.

But the tight coil exploded in a blast of raw, delirious sensation.

She screamed out her fulfilment as he shouted his own release, and collapsed with her into oblivion.

'I've never come that fast in my life.'

Issy stiffened at the muffled words next to her ear, the hazy afterglow shattering.

He was still buried deep inside her. Still firm, still semi-erect. His large frame anchoring her to the mattress.

She shoved his shoulder, tried to lower her legs—next to impossible with her thighs clasped tight around his hips. 'Let me up. I need to leave.' Now.

He lifted himself off her, and she stifled the groan as her swollen flesh released him with difficulty.

'What's wrong?' he murmured.

Was he joking?

They'd just had sex! Make that wild monkey sex. And they didn't even like each other. She closed her legs, curled away from him, the aching tenderness between her thighs a shameful reminder of the way they'd just ravaged each other.

It wasn't just wrong, it was insane. Forget ten years ago. This now classified as the biggest, most humiliating mistake of her life.

'Absolutely nothing,' she said caustically, the scent of sex suffocating her as she scooted over to the corner of the bed.

She sat up, ready to make a swift getaway, but one strong arm banded round her waist and dragged her back against a solid male chest.

Panic constricted around her throat. 'I really have to leave.'

'Settle down. Why are you in such a rush? You haven't got what you came for yet.'

'I…' She stuttered to a halt, his words slicing through the panic and cutting straight to the shame. 'I didn't…' She stopped, cleared her throat. The conversation they'd had before ripping each other's clothes off replaying in her mind at top volume.

She cringed. She hadn't meant to tell him she'd have sex with him for money, but somehow the desire, the need, the resentment had got all tangled up. And she had. Sort of.

Wild monkey sex had been bad enough, but adding in the money took things to a whole new level of sordid. 'The money wasn't the reason I...' She paused. Tried again to explain the unexplainable. 'I don't expect you to pay...'

His arm tightened. 'I know that, Issy. After what almost happened at the club, sex was inevitable.' He gave a rough chuckle. 'And, frankly, I'm insulted. I don't pay women for sex. Even you.'

She blinked. Furious at the sting of tears. 'Good, I'm glad you understand that,' she said, trying to regain a little dignity while she was stark naked and blushing like a beetroot.

She struggled. He held firm.

'Will you let go?' she demanded.

'What's the big hurry?' he said, his reasonableness starting to irritate her. 'Now we've got the sex out of the way, why shouldn't we talk about the money?'

Because I'd rather die on the spot.

She swung round, astonished at his blasé attitude. Was it really that easy for him to dismiss what they had done? Chalk it up to inevitability and forget about it?

She'd never had sex just to scratch an itch. Not until now anyway. She felt dreadful about it. Didn't he feel even a little bit ashamed about their behaviour?

Apparently not, from the easygoing look on his face.

She gripped the sheet in her fist. 'Yes, well, now we've got the sex out of the way...' How could he reduce everything to the lowest common denominator like that? 'I don't want to discuss anything else.' Because she, at least, had scruples. 'I need to get dressed. I'm getting a chill.'

Which was a blatant lie. She was the opposite of cold. The sun was blazing through the windows, and she could feel something that was still remarkably hard pressing against her bottom.

His hands stroked her tummy through the thin linen sheet, sending a shiver through her that had nothing to do with being chilled either.

'You can get dressed on one condition.' His breath whispered past her ear. 'That you don't run off.'

She nodded, so aroused again she would agree to tap dance naked to get out of his arms. Having to endure a conversation with him was by far the safer option, she decided as she dashed out of the bed.

To her consternation, he made no effort to get dressed himself, but simply relaxed back against the pillows, folded one arm behind his head and watched her. Ignoring him, she raced round the room in a crouch, with one arm banded across her breasts and the other covering what she could of her sex. Unfortunately she soon discovered that left her one crucial hand short to pick her bra and panties off the floor.

'Issy, what exactly are you doing?' Gio's amused voice rumbled from the bed.

She glanced round to find him staring at her, a puzzled smile on his face. 'I'm trying to maintain a little modesty. If that's okay with you,' she snapped.

Something he conspicuously lacked, she thought resentfully. With the sheet slung low on his hips, barely covering the distinctive bulge beneath, he looked as if he were auditioning for a banner ad in *Playgirl*.

'Isn't it a little late for that?' he said casually.

The blush burned as she concentrated on stepping into her knickers and fastening her bra behind her back one-handed.

She glared at him, having finally completed the tricky manoeuvres. 'Yes, I suppose it is. Thank you so much for pointing that out.'

Why did men always have to state the bloody obvious?

She turned away as he chuckled. Scouting around for her dress, she spotted it peeking out from under the bed. She whipped it off the floor and climbed into it, trying not to notice the torn seam caused by his eagerness to get the dress off her.

She then spent several agonising seconds trying to fasten the zip, with her arm twisted behind her back like a circus contortionist.

'Want some help with that?' His deep voice rumbled with amusement.

She huffed and gave in. The sooner she got dressed, the sooner she could get out of here.

She perched on the edge of the bed and presented her back to him. But instead of fastening the zip he swept the heavy curtain of hair over her shoulder and ran the pad of his thumb down the length of her neck.

'That's not helping,' she said, squeezing her thighs together as awareness ricocheted down her spine.

He chuckled as he tugged up the zip. He rested a warm palm on her bare shoulder. 'So how much money do you need?'

The softly asked question had a blast of guilt and despair drowning out her embarrassment.

The theatre!

What was she going to do now? Gio had been her last hope. Admittedly it hadn't been much of a hope, but she couldn't even ask him for the sponsorship now—it would make her look like a total tart, and anyway he wouldn't give it to her. Why should he?

'None,' she said, her mind reeling. How could she have been so reckless and irresponsible? 'Really, it'll be fine,' she murmured, her bottom lip quivering alarmingly

Don't you dare fall to pieces. Not yet.

She'd have to find another way. Somehow.

But as she went to stand he held her wrist. 'Why do I get the feeling you're lying?'

She looked down at the long, tanned fingers encircling her wrist. And suddenly felt like a puppy who had been given a good solid kick in the ribs.

'I'm not lying,' she said, alarmed by the quake in her voice. 'Everything's fine.'

He gripped her chin, forced her eyes to his. 'Issy, if you say everything's fine again I'm going to get seriously annoyed.' He pressed his thumb to her lip. 'I was there when you broke your wrist. Remember? You were twelve, and in a lot of pain, and yet you refused to shed a single tear. You look a lot closer to tears now. So there has to be a reason.'

She dipped her eyes to her lap, disturbed by the admiration in his voice—and the memory he'd evoked.

She hadn't cried that day, but she hadn't been particularly brave. The pain had seemed minimal once the sixteen-year-old Gio had discovered her in the grounds. He'd carried her all the way back to the Hall in his arms, the experience fuelling her fantasies for months and making her forget about her sore wrist as soon as he'd plucked her off the ground.

She brushed at her eyes with the heel of her hand. Gio's brusque tenderness that day was not something she needed to be thinking about right now.

'Maybe things aren't completely fine,' she said carefully. 'But I'll figure something out.'

He lifted a knee and slung his arm over it—edging that flipping sheet further south.

'That had better not mean more strip-a-grams,' he said.

'It *wasn't* a strip-a-gram,' she said, not appreciating the dictatorial tone. 'It was a singing telegram. There's a difference.'

'Uh-huh.' He didn't sound convinced. 'What's the money for? Are you in financial trouble?'

'Not me,' she murmured, her indignation forgotten. Strip-a-grams could well be the next step. 'It's the Crown and Feathers. The theatre pub I work for. I'm the general manager. I have been for the last four years. And we're about to be shut down by the bank.'

She stared at her hands, the enormity of the situation overwhelming her.

'All the people who work there and everyone in the local community who's helped us make the place a success will be devastated.' She blew out an unsteady breath, the truth hitting her hard in the solar plexus. 'And it's all my fault.'

She'd made a mess of everything. The fat lady was singing her heart out and, barring a miracle, there would be no shutting her up now.

* * *

Gio stared at Issy's pale shoulders rigid with tension, and at her slender hands clasped so tight in her lap she was probably about to dislocate a finger.

And wanted to punch his fist through a wall.

Why couldn't she have wanted the money for herself?

Of course she didn't. Issy didn't work that way. She'd always had too much integrity for her own good.

Now he didn't just feel responsible, he felt the unfamiliar prickle of guilt.

He shouldn't have goaded her. Made the money an issue.

But he hadn't been able to stop himself. The minute he'd spotted her waiting by the empty pool the desire he'd been trying and failing to handle for well over a week had surged back to life like a wild beast.

And he'd instantly resented it. And her.

She'd told him she detested him. Why did he still want her so much?

Suggesting she come up to his bedroom had been a ploy to humiliate her. He'd been sure she would refuse. But she hadn't. And her forthright acceptance had made him feel like a jerk.

Then she'd asked him for money. And resentment had turned to anger.

He'd seen the unconscious flare of desire in her eyes and decided to exploit it. She wasn't here for his money, and he could prove it.

The sex had been incredible. Better even than the first time. Explosive. Exhilarating. A force of nature neither of them could control.

And she'd enjoyed it as much as he had. So he'd been well and truly vindicated.

But her financial problems had ruined the nice buzz of triumph and spectacular sex, stabbing at his conscience in a way he didn't like.

'Exactly how much of a hole is your theatre in?' he asked.

'The interest on our loan is thirty thousand. And we've got less than two weeks to raise it.'

Her damp lashes made her turquoise eyes look even bigger than usual. And his conscience took another hit.

'Is that all?' he prompted.

She shook her head, looked back at her lap. 'We'd need over a hundred to be safe for the rest of the year.' She gave a jerky shrug, as if a huge weight were balanced on her shoulders. 'We've been trying to find sponsors for months now,' she continued. 'The two grants we got last year have been withdrawn. The pub revenue was hit by the smoking ban, and…' She trailed off, sighed. 'It was a stupid idea to come to you. Why should you care about some bankrupt theatre?' She brushed a single tear away. 'But I was desperate.'

He covered her clasped hands with one of his, surprised by the urge to comfort. 'Issy, stop crying.' He'd always hated to see her cry. 'The money's yours. All of it. It's not a problem.'

Her head lifted and she stared at him as if he'd just sprouted an extra head. 'Don't be silly. You can't do that. Why would you?'

He shrugged. 'Why wouldn't I? It's a good cause.' But even as he said it he knew that wasn't the reason he wanted to give her the money.

He'd never really forgiven himself for the way he'd stormed out on her all those years ago.

He didn't regret the decision to walk away. Issy had been young, romantic and impossibly sweet. She'd had a crush on him for years and didn't have a clue what he was really like. But he'd been much harder on her than he needed to be.

He'd accused her of keeping her virginity a secret. But he'd realised in hindsight that had been a stupid misunderstanding. She'd been too innocent to know they were talking at cross-purposes. But at the time he'd felt trapped and wary—and furious with himself for not withdrawing the instant he knew he was her first—and he'd taken it out on her.

Then she'd told him she loved him, and for one fleeting second he'd actually wanted it to be true—making him realise how much he had let his argument with the Duke get to him—and he'd taken that out on her too.

He wasn't about to explain himself now. Or ever. It was too late to apologise. But giving her the money would be a good way to make amends.

But as he looked into those luminous blue eyes the blood pounded back into his groin. And he realised he had a bigger problem to handle than any lingering sense of guilt.

Why hadn't the mind-blowing orgasm been enough?

'But you can't give me a hundred grand.' She pulled her hand out of his. 'That's a lot of money.'

'Do you want to save your theatre or not?' he replied impatiently. He wanted the money out of the way, so he could deal with the more pressing problem of how to re-establish control over his libido.

'Yes—yes, I do. But...' She trailed off.

'Then why are you trying to talk me out of this?'

'Because it's a hundred thousand pounds!'

'Issy, I spent close to that on my last car. It's not that much money. Not to me.'

Her eyebrows rose. 'I didn't know architecture was that lucrative.'

'It is when you do it right,' he said. And had to stifle the foolish desire to say a lot more.

He'd qualified two years early, beaten off a series of more experienced applicants to win a huge design competition, and then worked his backside off. And in the last three years it had paid off.

The Florence practice had won kudos around the world. He'd opened another office in Paris. Won a slew of prestigious architectural awards. And best of all he didn't have to bother entering competitions any more. The clients came to him. He was proud of how he'd managed to tame the destructiveness that had ruled his teenage years and turn his life around.

But he resisted the urge to launch into a list of his accomplishments. He didn't boast about his achievements. He didn't need anyone's approval. So why should he need Issy's?

'If it makes you feel better,' he began, 'I've been thinking of opening an office in London for a while.' Which wasn't exactly the truth. 'The Florence practice donates over a million euros to worthy causes every year. It's great PR and it keeps Luca, my tax accountant, happy.' Which *was* the truth. 'Sponsoring your theatre makes good business sense.'

She pressed her hands to her mouth, her eyes widening to saucer size. 'Oh. My. Lord. You're serious!' she shrieked, the decibel level muffled by her hands.

'You're actually going to give us the money.' She grasped his hand in both of hers. 'Thank you. Thank you. Thank you. You have no idea how much this means to me. And all the people who work at the Crown and Feathers.'

But he had a feeling he *did* know. And it made him feel uncomfortable. His reasons weren't exactly altruistic. And they were getting less altruistic by the second.

'I wish I knew how to thank you,' she said.

He almost told her it wasn't her thanks he wanted. But stopped himself because he'd just figured out what it was he did want.

He wanted Issy Helligan out of his system.

The girl and now the woman had been a fire in his blood for well over ten years. Why not admit it? He didn't fixate on women, but somehow he'd got fixated on her.

He'd tried walking away. He'd tried denial. And neither had worked.

Sorting out her financial troubles would finally put the guilt and responsibility from their past behind them. So why not take the next step? He had to return to Florence this afternoon, and he wanted Issy with him. So he could burn the fire out once and for all. Forget about her for good.

'There's only one snag,' he said, the white lie tripping off his tongue without a single regret.

No need to tell Issy about his plans yet.

She had a tendency to overreact, she was totally unpredictable, and she had a terrible track record for complicating sex with emotion. Better to get her to Florence first, and then deal with any fall-out.

'Oh, no—what?' she said, her face crumpling comically.

'You'll have to come to Florence with me. This afternoon.'

'To Florence?' She looked even more astonished than she had by the offer of money. But when he saw the flash of interest in her eyes he had a tough time keeping the smile of triumph off his face.

She needed this as much as he did. The only difference was she hadn't figured it out yet.

Issy tried to ignore the bubble of excitement under her breastbone. She had to get a grip on this thing... whatever it was. Now.

Maybe she could justify giving in to her hormones once, in the circumstances. She'd been stressed to the max in the last few months, hadn't dated in over a year, and Gio had always been able to short-circuit her common sense and make her yearn for things that weren't right for her. But she was *not* about to do the wild thing with him again. No matter what her body might want.

Gio was now officially the answer to the theatre's prayers. Which would make sex with him even more indefensible than it was already.

'Why?' she asked, hoping he wasn't about to suggest what she thought he was about to suggest.

'You need the money by next week, right?'

She nodded, still unable to believe that the theatre's problems could be solved so easily. And so completely.

'There's a ton of paperwork to sign, plus you may have to give a presentation to the board before I can release the money. It makes sense for you to come over. It shouldn't take more than a couple of days. The snag is, I'm leaving this afternoon. The helicopter's due here at two to take me to London City Airport, and then I'm taking the company jet back to Florence.'

'Oh, I see,' she murmured, disconcerted by the way the bubble had deflated at his businesslike tone. 'I'll ring my assistant Maxi. She can pack me a bag and meet us at City Airport. Don't worry. It's not a problem.'

This was good news. Fantastic news, in fact. Gio had committed to sorting out the theatre's financial situation. And she could think of worse things than spending a few days in Florence—especially after the hideous stress of the last few months. She had earned a break. And they could spare some of the theatre's money on a guesthouse now they were going to have plenty. She might even find time for some sightseeing.

'Arranging leave will be fine,' she said, managing to be businesslike and efficient at last. 'The sooner we can make it official the better.'

She and Gio probably wouldn't see that much of each other, she thought, dismissing the prickle of disappointment. 'Is it okay if I have a shower?' she asked, keeping her tone polite and impersonal.

'Go ahead and use the *en suite*,' he said, just as impersonally. 'I'll take the bathroom down the hall.'

But as she stepped into the bathroom she caught a glimpse of Gio's naked behind as he walked to his dresser, and realised her pheromones weren't being nearly as businesslike and efficient as the rest of her.

Gio grinned as the door to the *en suite* bathroom clicked closed. The offer to scrub her back had been close to irresistible. But he wasn't twenty-one any more—and he didn't plan to rush into anything he couldn't control. He would have to make sure Issy understood exactly what their little trip to Florence meant, and what it didn't, before he made his next move.

And once they'd got that settled he planned to indulge himself.

He pulled jeans and a T-shirt out of the dresser, listened to the gush of water from the shower and imagined Issy's lush, naked body slick with soapsuds.

After ten years, and two bouts of mind-blowing sex, he was finally going to get the chance to seduce Issy Helligan without anything between them. No guilt, no responsibility, no hurt feelings and preferably no clothes.

And he intended to savour every single second.

CHAPTER FIVE

'THAT guy's your Duke?' Maxi whispered loudly, as she passed Issy her battered wheel-around suitcase. Her eyes remained glued to Gio's retreating back as he disappeared into the sea of passengers at the airport's security checkpoint. 'How could you have kept *him* a secret all this time? I mean, look at that backside.'

'Max, close your mouth. You look like a guppy,' Issy said testily. After the strain of the last few hours she was feeling more than a little out of sorts—and she didn't want to deal with Maxi's regression into a fourteen-year-old schoolgirl.

Frankly, she was having enough trouble dealing with her own vivid fantasies about Gio. They'd done the wild thing. Once. And that had been quite enough. For both of them. So why couldn't she stop thinking about doing it again? Especially given that Gio had made it crystal-clear he wasn't in the market for a repeat performance.

After a twenty-minute shower she'd arrived downstairs, to find Gio in a meeting with the landscape architects and Jack Bradshaw assigned as her chaperon.

Jack had graciously invited her to share a buffet of

delicious antipasti dishes with the group of young architects and engineers working on the Hall project. But her stomach had tied itself in tight little knots as she'd fielded a barrage of questions from Gio's team about their shared childhood at the Hall. Did they all know about her private appointment in his bedroom earlier? If only he could put in an appearance so she didn't have to deal with their avid curiosity all on her own.

But Gio hadn't appeared. Thankfully Jack had whisked her off on a tour of the Hall after lunch, so she hadn't had too much time to examine why she felt so disappointed.

It hadn't stopped the strange and inexplicable feelings that had sprung to the surface as she and Jack had strolled through her childhood home and he'd pointed out all Gio's improvements. She hadn't needed Jack's running commentary. She'd seen for herself the remarkable changes he'd made. And the tight little knots of disappointment and embarrassment had quickly turned to giant knots of confusion as she marvelled at the brilliance and artistry of Gio's redesign.

The forbidding, cramped and suffocating rooms had been turned into light, airy spaces by knocking down partition walls and reinstating windows that had been boarded up. Old carpets had been ripped out to reveal beautiful inlaid mosaic flooring, a new staircase had been constructed using traditional carpentry to open up the second floor, and the grimly unappealing below stairs kitchen had been turned into a state-of-the art catering space any master chef would have been proud of by digging out the basement and adding yet more light with a domed atrium.

Gio had brought the Hall back from the dead. But, more than that, he'd given it a new lease of life. And she couldn't help wondering why he would have gone to all this trouble.

He'd left the Hall all those years ago, and to her knowledge had never come back. Not once bothering to contact his father or even attend the Duke's funeral. She'd always thought he hated this place, so why had he restored it so sensitively? Had he wanted to prove something?

And why couldn't she shake the odd feeling of pride in his achievements? What Gio had done to his father's house had nothing whatsoever to do with her.

The helicopter ride to London had gone smoothly enough; the noise in the cabin making it impossible for them to speak without shouting. Gio had worked on his laptop and she hadn't disturbed him, even though a million and one questions about the Hall and what he'd done to it had kept popping into her head.

This was a business trip. And she had to keep it that way. Asking Gio questions about his motivations for restoring the Hall felt too personal.

Unfortunately, every time his thigh had brushed against the silk of her dress, or his elbow had bumped hers on the armrest, business was the last thing on her mind. And by the time they'd arrived at City Airport and been whisked into the terminal building, Issy's hormones had been cartwheeling like Olympic gymnasts.

She'd only had a moment to introduce Gio to Maxi, and watch her friend gush all over him, before he'd excused himself again, explaining that he had a few calls to make and would meet her on the plane.

The ludicrous thing was, she was starting to get a

bit of a complex about how eager he seemed to ignore her. Which was totally idiotic. She didn't need his attention. Or want it. It would only encourage her cartwheeling hormones.

Maxi's excited chatter wasn't helping. Reminding her of all the giggly conversations she'd once had about Gio in her teens.

'How do you know him?' Maxi asked, still gushing like his number one fan. 'It's obvious there's a connection between you. Is that why he offered to fund the theatre?' Maxi turned wide eyes on her. 'You're having a fling, aren't you?'

Colour flushed into Issy's cheeks. 'We are not,' she said, pretty sure one bout of wild monkey sex didn't count. 'We grew up together. He's an old friend.'

Maxi's eyes narrowed. 'Then why are you going to Florence with him? And why are you blushing?'

'I'm not blushing,' she lied, cursing her pale skin. 'And I have to go to Florence to sign the sponsorship papers. It's just a formality. I told you that.'

'Iss, don't get me wrong,' Maxi said, putting on her sincere face and grating on Issy's nerves even more. 'I think it's fab that he's taking you to Florence. You absolutely deserve a break. Especially with someone as tasty as that. You don't have to pretend with me. We're mates.' She nudged Issy's shoulder. 'And I'll give Dave and the troops the official story, I promise.' She smiled. 'So, how long have you two been an item?'

Good grief.

Issy yanked up the handle on her suitcase. 'It's not an official story. It's the truth.'

'Oh, come on,' Maxi scoffed. 'Let's examine the

evidence here,' she said in her no-nonsense voice. The one Issy usually appreciated. 'First off: no one needs to travel anywhere to sign a few papers these days, because it can all be done by e-mail.' She began to count off points on her fingers. 'Second: it's obvious you've had a shower in the last few hours, because your hair has started to frizz at the ends.'

Issy touched her hair self-consciously, remembering how observant Maxi was.

'And then there's the rip in the back of your dress to account for.'

Far *too* observant.

'And, last but by no means least,' Maxi continued, 'there's the way he looked at you just now.'

'What way?'

'Like he wanted to devour you in one quick bite.'

Okay, that was an observation too far. Gio had gone out of his way to avoid her for the last two hours. She ought to know. She had the inferiority complex to prove it.

'No, he didn't.'

'Yes, he did.' Maxi's quick grin had Issy blinking. 'I saw him. Those dreamy brown eyes went all sexy and intense, and he stared at you so long even I started to get excited. And I'm just an innocent bystander. If you aren't already having a hot, passionate fling with that guy, you should be.'

'But that's...' She sputtered to a stop, embarrassingly excited herself now. 'That's not possible.'

'Why not?'

'Because...' Her mind went totally blank as her hormones cartwheeled off a cliff.

'Miss Helligan? Mr Hamilton has asked me to escort you through Security.'

Issy turned to find a man in a flight attendant's uniform hovering at her elbow.

'Right. Fine.'

Please, God, don't let him have heard any of that.

She gave Maxi a quick hug. 'I've got my mobile if you need to call. But I'll check in tonight when I know where I'm staying. Give Dave and the troops the good news. And see if you can't locate the—'

'Issy, stop organising and go. Everything's under control.' Maxi squeezed her extra hard. 'Be sure to give His Grace my extra special thanks,' she whispered wiggling her eyebrows suggestively. 'And please feel free to do anything I wouldn't do.'

Issy shot her a hard stare, but couldn't think of a thing to say that would sound remotely convincing. It seemed she had some serious thinking to do—because her trip to Florence had just got a great deal more dangerous.

'This way, Miss Helligan. Mr Hamilton is waiting for you on the plane.'

Issy tried to take stock of the situation as the flight attendant led her past the endless queue snaking towards the security checkpoint.

'But what about passport control and security?' she asked, trailing behind him.

Did none of the usual headaches of air travel apply to a man with Gio's lifestyle?

But as she followed her battered suitcase through the door the attendant held open, and watched it being whisked through an X-ray machine by her own personal security official, it occurred to her that Gio's wealth and success were the least of her worries.

Mounting the metal steps of a sleek silver jet with the GH Partnership logo emblazoned on its tail, she tried to think rationally.

She'd planned to be in complete control here. But she wasn't. This was supposed to be a business trip. Plain and simple. Nothing more. Nothing less. But what if it wasn't?

Gio stepped out of the pilot's cabin as she boarded the plane—and she felt a traitorous thrill shoot through her. He looked relaxed and in control as he leaned against the metal portal, folded his arms over his chest and let his eyes wander over her figure. His casual attire of jeans and a faded T-shirt were at odds with the jet's luxury leather seats and thick pile carpeting, but they reminded her of the reckless, rebellious boy.

But he wasn't that boy any more. He was a man. A wildly successful, dangerously sexy man she'd agreed to go to Florence with. His gaze drifted back to her face. Make that a wildly successful, dangerously sexy man with a very predatory gleam in his eye.

How could she not have spotted that earlier?

'Hello, Isadora,' he said, his voice a husky murmur. 'Ready for lift-off?'

Her nipples puckered into bullet points, her toes curled in her pumps—and she wondered if he was talking in euphemisms just to annoy her.

Ignoring the flush working its way up her neck, she decided to wrestle back some control. He'd bulldozed her into this. It was about time she found out exactly what was going on.

'Is there really any paperwork to sign in Florence?'

He rubbed his jaw. 'Now, why would you ask that?'

he said as the predatory gleam went laser-sharp. And she knew she'd been had.

'This has all been a set-up, hasn't it? But why…?' Her indignation cut off as the blood drained out of her face. 'The sponsorship? That wasn't a joke too, was it?'

'You can cut the drama queen act.' He chuckled, stepped towards her. 'I've already spoken to Luca and the money will be transferred tomorrow, once you give him your bank details.'

Her relief was short-lived as indignation surged back. 'So why am I going to Florence?'

He placed his hands on her hips, his eyes darker than the devil's. 'Why don't you take a wild guess?'

'I've got a better idea.' She braced her palms against his chest. 'Why don't you give me a straight answer?'

'All right, then,' he said, not remotely chastened. 'I plan to spend a few days ravaging you senseless.'

'Ravaging…' Her jaw went slack as fire spiked her cheeks and roasted her sex. 'Are you insane?'

The smug smile got bigger. 'Stop pretending to be outraged. Once wasn't enough. And you know it.'

A sharp reprimand rose up in her throat, but got choked off when his fingers sank into her hair and his lips covered hers in a hungry, demanding kiss.

She pushed him away, clinging onto the last edge of sanity. 'I'm not doing this. It's…' *What?* 'A very bad idea.'

'Why?'

'It just is.' If he gave her a moment she could probably come up with a thousand reasons. Just because she couldn't think of any right this second…

His hands caressed her scalp, making it hard for her

to think straight. 'Issy, the past's over,' he murmured. 'But if you're still hung up on—'

'Of course I'm not,' she cut in. 'This has nothing to do with our past.' She pulled out of his arms. 'And everything to do with your unbelievable arrogance. How dare you trick me into coming to Florence? When exactly were you going to tell me about your plans to ravage me senseless?'

His lips quirked some more. 'I'm telling you now.'

'Well, that's not good enough. What if I want to say no?'

He drew a thumb down her cheek, his eyes black with arousal. 'And do you?'

Even as the denial formed in her mind, it was muted by the long, liquid pull low in her belly. 'No...I mean, yes,' she said, scrambling to keep a firm grip on her indignation.

His palm settled on her nape. 'Let's finish what we started.' His thumb stroked her throat, stoking the fire at her core. 'Then we can both move on.'

Could it really be that simple? Was this thing between them just left-over sexual chemistry?

But even as she tried to make sense of her feelings he tugged her towards him and took her mouth in another mind-numbing kiss.

Her fingers curled into the cotton of his T-shirt, but this time she couldn't find the will to push him away. The pent-up hunger of only a few hours ago burst free as her tongue tangled with his.

He drew back first, the slow smile melting the last of her resistance. 'No ties. No strings. Just some great sex and then we go our separate ways. It's your choice. If you can't handle it, we part now. I'm not interested in anything serious.'

'I'm perfectly well aware of your commitment problems,' she countered.

Not only did she have personal experience, but when she'd been Googling him yesterday she'd found numerous paparazzi shots of him with supermodels and starlets and society princesses on his arm. And not one photo of him with the same woman twice. The man's track record when it came to relationships sucked. Any fool could see that.

'As long as that's understood,' he said easily, clearly not insulted in the least, 'I don't see a problem.' The sensual smile made the heat pound harder. 'Florence is spectacular at this time of year, and I have a villa in the hills where we can satisfy all our prurient sexual fantasies. And, believe me, after ten years I've stored up quite a few.' He threaded his fingers into her hair, pushed the heavy curls away from her face. 'We had fun together when we were kids, Issy. We could have more fun now.'

Issy swallowed, the rough feel of his palm on her cheek making the promise of pleasure all but irresistible. 'And the theatre's sponsorship will be okay either way?' she clarified, desperate not to get swept away on a sea of lust too soon.

He gave his head a small shake. 'I already told you—'

'Okay. Yes,' she interrupted, placing her hands on his shoulders. 'I accept.'

Gio was dangerous. Yes. But danger could be thrilling as well as frightening. And right now the thrill was winning. Big-time. She felt like Alice, tumbling head first into Wonderland. Exhilarated, excited, and totally terrified.

His arms banded around her waist. 'Good.'

Issy had bounced up on her toes, eager to seal their devil's bargain, when she heard a gruff chuckle from behind them.

'You'll have to save that for later, Hamilton,' said an unfamiliar voice.

She jerked round, spotting a stout, older man in a pilot's uniform.

'Our slot's in ten minutes,' the man said, sending her an indulgent smile. 'I'm sorry, miss, but we need to do the final equipment check.'

Gio swore softly, touched his forehead to hers, then stepped to one side. 'Issy, this is James Braithwaite,' he said, keeping his arm round her waist. 'Co-pilot and all-round killjoy.'

Issy shook the man's hand before her foggy brain registered the information. 'Did you say co-pilot?'

'That's right,' Gio said nonchalantly, giving her a quick kiss on the nose and letting her go. 'You'd better get strapped in.'

'Wait a minute.' Issy held his arm, her fingers trembling. 'You're not flying this thing yourself?'

The sleek jet suddenly morphed into a metallic death trap. Images flashed through her mind of Gio as a teenager after he'd totalled his father's vintage Bentley, or Gio on his motorbike with her clinging on the back, shooting around blind bends at twenty miles above the speed limit.

Okay, maybe she could risk a quick fling with Gio, to finish what they'd started this afternoon, but she wasn't about to risk her life letting him fly her any-where. The boy had always had a need for too much speed and far too little caution. On the evidence so far, she wasn't convinced the man was any less reckless.

Gio grinned at her horrified expression. 'Oh, ye of little faith,' he murmured. 'I happen to be a qualified pilot, Isadora. With a good solid one hundred hours of flying time under my belt.' His smile widened as he stroked her cheek, weakening her resolve, not to mention her thigh muscles. 'Trust me. You're perfectly safe in my hands.'

As she strapped herself into her seat and watched him duck into the pilot's cabin, Issy knew she'd be mad to trust Gio Hamilton with anything.

But forewarned was forearmed. And, given how well aware she was of Gio's shortcomings, she was more than capable of keeping herself safe this time.

After a smooth take-off, and an even smoother touch down in Pisa two hours later, Issy had to concede Gio could be trusted to pilot an aircraft without plummeting her to earth. But when he ushered her just as smoothly into an open-topped Ferrari at the airport, then sped her through miles of glorious sun-drenched Italian countryside, her pulse continued to thump like a sledgehammer and she knew she shouldn't trust him with anything else.

The noise of the wind and the rush of the heart-stopping scenery meant they couldn't talk during the drive. Which gave Issy more than enough time to think.

Was what she had agreed to do demeaning? After all, what self-respecting smart, capable career woman agreed to be ravaged senseless?

But after examining their arrangement Issy came to

the conclusion she didn't have a choice. Because Gio was right. She needed to get over the dirty trick her hormones had been playing on her for years.

She'd had a measly two proper boyfriends since Gio had introduced her to the joys of sex. And both relationships had ended with a whimper rather than a bang. At the time she'd told herself it was because she wasn't ready, because the timing hadn't been right, because the two guys she'd dated hadn't been right for her. But now she knew the truth.

That special spark, that frisson of sexual energy that had exploded in her face today had always been missing. Sex wasn't the *most* important thing in a relationship. She knew that. But it wasn't unimportant either. She'd compared Johnny and Sam to Gio in bed without even knowing it, and found them wanting. Maybe it was some sort of natural selection, a mating instinct thing— after all Gio was the ultimate alpha male in the sack— or maybe it was just that Gio had been her first. But whatever the problem was it needed to be dealt with.

Because if she didn't deal with it she might never be able to form a long-term committed relationship with anyone, ever. The sort of relationship she'd spent her girlhood dreaming about. The sort of relationship her parents had shared before her father's early death. The sort of relationship she'd almost given up hope of ever being able to find for herself.

This wasn't about letting Gio ravage her senseless— it was about releasing her from the sexual hold he had always had over her, ever since that first night, and allowing her to forget about him so she would be free to find the *real* one true love of her life.

Convinced she'd satisfied all her concerns about the trip, Issy couldn't understand why her pulse refused to settle down during the drive. In fact it was still working overtime when Gio steered the Ferrari off a narrow cobbled road in the hills around the city and onto a tree-lined drive.

The scent of lemon trees perfumed the air as he braked in front of a picture-perfect Florentine villa constructed of dusky pink terracotta stone. A grand fountain with two naked water nymphs entwined at its centre tinkled quietly in the circular forecourt.

Issy gawped as Gio leapt effortlessly out of the low-slung car.

She wasn't a stranger to wealth and privilege, for goodness' sake. She'd spent the formative years of her life living below stairs in a stately home. So why had her pulse just skipped into overdrive?

He opened the car door. As she stepped onto the pebbled drive she had to remind herself to breathe.

The carved oak entrance door swung open as they approached. A middle-aged woman with a homely face and a pretty smile bowed her head and introduced herself in Italian as Carlotta. Gio introduced Issy in turn, and then had a conversation with the housekeeper before she excused herself.

Hearing Gio speak Italian had Issy's heartbeat kicking up another notch.

How strange. Even though he spoke English with barely a hint of an accent, Issy knew he was fluent in Italian. But there was something about hearing the language flow so fluidly, watching him use his hands for emphasis, that made him seem very sophisticated and

European—as far removed from the surly boy she remembered as it was possible to get.

She tried to shake off her uneasiness and calm her frantic heartbeat, but as Gio led her through a series of increasingly beautiful rooms the unsettled feeling only got worse.

The house's furnishings were few, but suited the open Mediterranean layout and looked hand-crafted and expensive. The minimalist luxury should have made the place seem exclusive and unapproachable, but it didn't. As they walked into a wide, open-plan living area, the brightly coloured rugs, the lush, leafy potted plants and the stacks of dog-eared architectural magazines on the coffee table gave its elegance a lived-in feel, making the house seem unpretentious and inviting.

Gio held open a glass door at the end of the room and beckoned her forward.

Issy stepped on to a balcony which looked across the valley past a steeply terraced garden. At the bottom of the hill in the distance the sluggish Arno River wound its way through Florence, the city laid out below them like a carpet of wonders. She could make out the Ponte Vecchio to her right, probably heaving with tourists in the sweltering afternoon heat, and appreciated the citrus-perfumed breeze even more. Walking to the low stone wall that edged the terrace, she spotted a large pool in the lawned garden one level below, its crystal blue waters sparkling in the sunshine.

'Goodness,' she whispered, as her heartbeat pounded in her ears.

Who would have expected the wild, reckless boy

whom she had assumed would never settle anywhere to make himself a home almost too beautiful to be real?

'So what do you think?' he asked.

She turned to find him standing behind her, studying her, his hands tucked into the back pockets of his jeans. She thought she saw a muscle in his jaw tense. As if he were anxious about what she might say.

Don't be an idiot.

He didn't care what she thought. That had to be a trick of the light. He knew how amazing this place was. And she knew perfectly well she was only one in a very long line of women he'd invited here.

Don't you dare start analysing every little nuance of his behaviour, you ninny. Reading things into it that aren't there.

She cleared her throat. 'I think you have incredible taste.' She stared out at the breathtaking view. 'And calling this place a villa doesn't do it justice. I think paradise would be more appropriate.'

'It'll do for now,' he said casually.

His palms settled on her waist. Tugging her back against his chest, he nuzzled the sensitive skin below her ear. 'Although, given what I'm thinking right now, paradise lost would be the best choice.'

She gasped out a laugh, finding it hard to breathe as brutal realisation hit her. Being in Gio's home would involve an intimacy she hadn't bargained on during all her careful justifications.

'Why don't we go check out the master bedroom?' he said, the humour doing nothing to mask his intentions. He folded his arms around her waist, making her breasts feel heavy and tender as he drew her into a hard hug. 'I'd love to know what you think of the…' He paused provocatively, nipping her earlobe. 'View…'

She pictured the view the last time they'd been naked together. And the hot, heavy weight in her belly pulsed. Panic spiked at the vicious throb of desire.

I'm not ready for this. Not yet.

She whipped round to face him, breaking his hold. 'Could we go sightseeing?' she said, trying not to wince at the high-pitched note in her voice.

She couldn't dive back into bed with him. Not straight away. Sex was one thing, intimacy another, and she couldn't afford to confuse the two.

His brows rose up his forehead. 'You want to go sightseeing? Seriously?'

'Yes, please. I adore sightseeing,' she said, keeping her voice as firm as possible to disguise the lie. She could feel his arousal against her hip and eased back a step. 'I've never been to Florence. I'm dying to see as much of it as I can. Could we eat in the city tonight?' A couple of hours to establish some distance. That was all she needed. She was sure of it. 'I've never been to Italy before,' she rattled on, pretending not to notice the frown on his face. 'And I've heard Florence has some of the best *trattorias* in Italy.'

What the…?

Gio knew a delaying tactic when he heard one. And Issy's sudden transformation into super-tourist definitely qualified. He spotted the rigid peaks of her breasts beneath her dress, the staggered rise and fall of her breathing—and almost howled with frustration.

Hadn't they settled all this on the plane?

He was ready to get to the main event now. More than ready. In fact, if he hadn't been co-piloting the plane he would have got to it sooner, giving in to the temptation to initiate her into the Mile-High Club.

Thrusting his hands into his pockets, he kept his face carefully blank. Her cheeks were a bright rosy pink but he could see the alarm on her face.

He should have guessed things wouldn't be that straightforward, because nothing ever was with Issy. She'd been jumpy ever since they'd walked into the house. He'd enjoyed her nerves at first. Keeping Issy off-kilter was a good way to handle her. And it hadn't done his ego any harm to see how impressed she was with his home.

But when she'd turned round, her eyes wide with surprise, he'd had the strangest sensation she could see right through him. And for the first time in his life he'd wanted to ask a woman what she was thinking.

Not that he intended to do it. For one thing, straight answers were not Issy's forte. And for another, he had a golden rule against asking women personal questions. Once you opened that floodgate it was impossible to slam it shut again.

He'd already broken one golden rule by inviting her into his home. He generally avoided getting into any kind of routine with the women he dated.

'Sure. No problem.' He forced his shoulders to relax.

If Issy wanted to play hard to get for an evening, why not let her? He could slow the pace for a few hours. If he had to.

'I know a place not far from the Piazza della Repubblica. Their *bistecca fiorentina*'s like a religion.'

And Latini had the sort of low-key, unpretentious atmosphere that should relax her while still being classy enough to impress her.

He would ply her with a couple of glasses of their Chianti Classico, comfort-feed her the Florentine speciality and indulge in a spot of light conversation. Maybe he'd even show her a few of the sights. Keep things easy. He could do that. For an evening.

'Are you sure?' she said, sounding surprised but looking so relieved he smiled.

'Yeah. It'll be fun,' he said, forcing down his frustration. He could wait a while longer to get her naked. He wasn't *that* desperate.

Then a thought struck him, and he realised he could make it more fun than he'd figured. He smiled some more. 'We can take the Vespa. My mechanic Mario gave it an overhaul recently, so it's running fairly well for once.'

'A scooter?' She had the same shocked look he'd seen on the plane. 'You ride a scooter? That sounds a bit incongruous for a duke.'

'Now, Isadora.' He brushed a thumb across her cheekbone. 'I hope you're not saying I'm a snob?' he teased as her cheeks pinkened prettily. 'No Florentine with a brain takes a car into the city. A scooter is the only way to go.'

And, like all natives, he drove his Vespa at breakneck speed. Which meant she'd have to glue herself to him to stop from falling off.

His grin got bigger as his gaze flicked down her outfit. 'If you've got some jeans, you might want to put them on. The staff will have put your suitcase in the master bedroom.' Placing his hands on her shoulders, he directed her towards a wrought-iron staircase at the end of the terrace. 'Take those stairs and the door's at the end of the balcony. I'll get the Vespa out of the garage and meet you out front.'

By the time they got back here, he'd have her naked soon enough.

Mounting the stairs to the upper balcony, Issy watched Gio stroll across the terrace, those damn denims hugging his gorgeous butt like a second skin.

She dragged her gaze away and took a moment to admire the almost as phenomenal view of Florence at dusk. In the enormous bedroom suite she slipped into jeans and a simple white wraparound blouse, and stared at the king-size mahogany bed dominating the room. The reckless thrill cascading through her body at the thought of what the nights and days ahead would hold had the hot, heavy feeling turning to aching need.

She huffed out a breath.

Okay, abstinence had never been an option. Not where Gio was concerned. He was too irresistible. And trying to distract him from the inevitable would only end up frustrating them both.

But that did not mean he got to have everything his own way. He'd railroaded her into boarding that plane, then exploited the hunger between them to get exactly what he wanted. Mindless sex with no strings attached.

Well, fine, she didn't want any strings either. But it wasn't as easy for her to simply dismiss their past. And she wasn't quite as adept at separating sex from intimacy, the way he was. And the reason why was simple. She'd never had sex with a stranger before. Or not intentionally. But she could see now that was exactly what Gio was. Now.

Finding a lavish *en suite* bathroom, she spent a few extra minutes brushing out her hair, washing her face and reapplying her make-up. And struggling to slow the rapid ticks of her heartbeat.

She'd once believed she knew Gio and understood him. And from there it had been one short step into love.

After that first night she'd always thought the reasons why she'd been so foolish were simple. She'd been young and immature and in desperate need of male approval. She'd lost her father at an early age, and it had left an aching hole in the centre of her life that couldn't be filled. Until Gio had appeared, a sad, surly but magnetic boy, who had seemed to need her as much as she needed him.

But now she could see there had been another, less obvious reason why she'd fallen in love with a figment of her own imagination.

Even when they were children there had been an air of mystery about Gio. He'd always been so guarded and cautious about any kind of personal information.

She had talked endlessly about her hopes and dreams, about her mum, about her schoolfriends, even about the shows she liked to watch on TV. Gio had listened to her chatter, but had said virtually nothing about his own life, his own hopes and dreams in return. She'd never even had an inkling he was interested in design. No wonder she had been so surprised about his success as an architect.

And then there had been the wall of silence surrounding the ten months of the year he spent in Rome, with his mother.

As a teenager, Issy had been totally in awe of Claudia Lorenzo—like every other girl her age. A flamboyant and stunningly beautiful bit-part actress, who had fought her way out of the Milan slums, Gio's mother had reinvented herself as a fashion icon, gracing the pages of *Vogue* and *Vanity Fair* while on a merry-go-round of affairs and marriages with rich, powerful men. Not all that surprisingly, Issy had quizzed Gio mercilessly about 'La Lorenzo' in her early teens.

But Gio had always refused to talk about his mother. So Issy had eventually stopped asking, conjuring up all sorts of romantic reasons why he should keep his life in Rome a secret.

Issy squared her shoulders and ran unsteady palms down the stiff new denim of her jeans. Why not use this week to dispel that air of mystery. To finally satisfy her curiosity about Gio? She'd always wanted to know why Gio kept so many secrets and why he seemed so determined never to have a permanent relationship. Once she had her answer, his power to fascinate her, to tantalise her, would be gone for good.

Gio was unlikely to co-operate, of course—being as guarded now as he had ever been—and it would be hard not to get sidetracked while indulging in all the physical pleasures and revelling in the sights, sounds and tastes of the beautiful Tuscan capital.

But luckily for her she was a master at multi-tasking, and she never backed down from a challenge. Skills she'd perfected while running the theatre and handling everything from actors' egos to imminent bankruptcy. Why not put those skills to good use?

So she could enjoy everything the next few days

had to offer. Get over her addiction to Gio's superstar abilities in bed. And finally get complete closure on all the mistakes of her past.

CHAPTER SIX

'So why are you so petrified of commitment?'

Gio choked on the expensive Chianti he'd been sipping, so surprised by Issy's probing question he had to grab his napkin to catch the spray. He put the glass down on the restaurant's white linen tablecloth, next to the remains of the mammoth T-bone steak they'd shared. 'Issy, I've just eaten about a half pound of rare beef. What are you trying to do? Give me indigestion?' he said, only half joking.

Where had that come from?

Everything had been going surprisingly well till now. Their sightseeing trip had been less of a chore than he'd expected. Issy had always been sexy as hell, but he'd forgotten how refreshing, funny and forthright she was too.

Perhaps because she was still a little jumpy, she'd hardly stopped talking since they'd left the villa, but rather than annoying him the mostly one-sided conversation had brought back fond memories from their childhood. For a boy who had been taught as soon as he could speak that it was better to keep his mouth shut, listening to Issy talk had made him feel blissfully normal. Having her chatter wash over him again tonight had reminded him how much he'd once enjoyed just listening to her speak.

The only time she'd been silent was when he'd whipped his classic Vespa through the streets of Florence with her clinging on like a limpet. Which had brought back another more visceral memory of that first wild ride aboard his motorbike.

After that he'd needed a distraction. Her warm breasts pressing against his back had not done a great deal for his self-control. So he'd had the inspired idea of taking her on a private tour of the Uffizi while he cooled off. But as they'd walked hand in hand through the darkened Vasari gallery and she'd peppered him with questions, a strange thing had happened. He'd watched Issy's face light up when she took in the Renaissance splendour of Boticelli's *Primavera*, heard her in-drawn breath at the ethereal beauty of Titian's *Venus*, and he'd really started to enjoy himself.

He'd taken a few dates here before, but none of them had been as awestruck and excited by the beauty of the art as Issy.

When they'd got to Latini for a late dinner, Issy had devoured the rich, succulent Tuscan speciality with the same fervour. But, as he'd watched her lick the rich gravy from her full bottom lip, enjoyment and nostalgia had turned sharply to anticipation.

As much as he'd enjoyed Issy's company over the last few hours, her avid appreciation of the art and her entertaining abilities as a conversationalist, he didn't want to talk any more. And especially not about his least favourite subject.

But before he could think of a subtle way to change the subject, she started up again.

'You're always so adamant you don't do permanent. You don't do the long-haul,' she said, looking him straight in the eye. 'Don't you think that's a bit peculiar? Especially for a man of your age?'

'I'm only thirty-one,' he said, annoyed. It wasn't as if he were about to pick up his pension.

'I know, but isn't that when most men are thinking of settling down? Having kids?'

That did it. Forget subtle—he wasn't having this conversation. No way. 'Why do you care? Unless you're angling for a proposal?' he said, a bit too forcefully.

Instead of looking hurt or offended, she laughed. 'Stop being so conceited. A man with your commitment problems is hardly the catch of the century.'

'That's good to know,' he grumbled, not as pleased as he would have expected by the off-hand remark.

Propping her elbow on the table, she leaned into her palm and gazed at him. 'I'm just really curious. What happened to make you so dead set against having a proper relationship?'

'I *have* proper relationships,' he said, not sure why he was defending himself. 'What do you call this?'

She giggled, her deep blue eyes sparkling mischievously in the candlelight. 'An *improper* relationship.'

'Very funny,' he said wryly as blood pounded into his groin.

Signalling the waiter, he asked for the bill in Italian. As the man left, laden with their empty plates, Gio topped up their wine glasses. 'Let's go back to the villa for dessert,' he said. Time to stop debating this nonsense and start debating which part of her he planned to feast on first. 'And discuss *how* improper.'

Seeing the heat and the determination on his face, Issy struggled to keep the simmering passion at bay that she was sure he'd been stoking all evening.

Every time his fingers cupped her elbow, every time his palm settled on the small of her back, every time his breath brushed across her earlobe as he whispered some amusing story or anecdote in her ear, or his chocolate gaze raked over her figure, her arousal had kicked up another notch. And she was sure he knew it.

But she wasn't going to be distracted that easily. Not yet anyway.

'What's the matter, Gio. Don't you *know* why you can't maintain a relationship?'

He drummed his fingers on the table, the rhythmic taps doing nothing to diminish the intensity in those melted chocolate eyes. 'It's not that I can't,' he replied. 'It's that I don't want to.' He leaned forward, placed his elbows on the table, a confident smile curving his lips. 'Why would I bother if it will never work?'

'What makes you think that?' she asked, stunned by the note of bitterness.

'People get together because of animal attraction,' he said, adding a cynical tilt to his smile. 'But that doesn't last. Eventually they hate each other, even if they pretend not to.' He took her wrist off the table, skimmed his thumb across the pulse-point. 'It's human nature. Relationships are about sex. You can dress it up with hearts and flowers if you want. But I choose not to.'

Issy sucked in a breath, shocked by the conviction in his voice and a little hurt by the brittle, condescending tone.

The evening so far had been magical. So magical she had been lulled into a false sense of companionship to go with the heady sexual thrill.

From the moment Gio's vintage scooter had careered down the steep cobbled hill into the city, his rock-hard abs tensing beneath her fingertips and the wind catching her hair, the sexual thrill had shot into her bloodstream like a drug. She was in Florence with a devastatingly handsome man who knew how to play her erogenous zones like a virtuoso. Why not ride the high?

But as the evening wore on it wasn't just the promise of physical pleasure that excited her.

Their first stop had been the world-famous Uffizi art gallery, where an eager young architectural student who worked as a night-guard and obviously idolised Gio had ushered them into a veritable cave of wonders of Italian art treasures.

Gio had taken courses in art history as part of his degree, and hadn't seemed to mind answering her endless questions. He'd regaled her with fascinating stories about the paintings on display, and talked about his love of art and architecture with a knowledge and passion so unlike the reticence she remembered about him as a boy it had captivated her.

When they'd stepped out of the gallery, darkness had fallen, the cloaking spell of evening giving the city a new and enchanting vibrancy. The tourists had all but disappeared, no doubt retiring to their hotels after a day spent sightseeing in the merciless August heat, and the locals had reclaimed their streets. Crowds of young, stylish Florentines, posing and gesticulating, spilled out of bars and cafés into cramped alleyways and grand *piazzas*, illuminated by neon and lamplight. As she'd clung on to Gio and watched Florence and its inhabitants whip past, Issy had been assailed by a powerful sense of belonging. Tonight, with Gio beside her, it didn't seem to matter that she didn't speak a word of Italian and couldn't have looked less Mediterranean if she tried. She knew it was a fanciful notion, conjured by the city's enchanting allure, but it had brought with it a buzz of anticipation to complement the desire coursing through her veins.

What if she and Gio could become friends again, as well as lovers, during their weekend of debauchery?

The meal had been equally glorious. The small but packed *trattoria* wore its centuries-old history on its smoke-stained walls and in the sensational tastes and textures of its signature dish. Gio was clearly a regular. The head waiter had clapped him on the back and led them to the only table which wasn't communal as soon as they'd arrived.

Issy suspected Gio had entertained hundreds of other women here before, but she refused to care. This was a few days out of time for both of them. A chance not just to indulge in the intense physical attraction between them, but maybe also to renew the precious childhood companionship they'd once shared before misunderstandings and maturity—and one night of misguided sex—had destroyed it.

But how could they do that if Gio insisted on shutting her out and treating her as if her view on love and relationships was beneath contempt?

Maybe she'd been young and foolish at seventeen, and she'd certainly made an enormous mistake picking Gio as her Mr Right, but she intended to carry on looking—and she resented him implying that made her an imbecile.

She tugged her hand out of his. 'That's all very interesting, Gio. But what about love? What about when you find the person you want to spend the rest of your life with?'

'You don't still believe that's going to happen, do you?' he said with an incredulous laugh.

'Yes, I do. It happens all the time. It was exactly like that for my parents,' she said with passion, her temper mounting. 'They adored each other. My mum still talks about my dad, and he's been dead for twenty-one years.'

'If you say so,' he said, sounding sceptical. 'But that would make *your* parents the exception, not the rule.'

She heard the tinge of regret, not quite drowned out by his condescension, and her temper died. 'What makes you think your parents aren't the exception?'

He stiffened at the quiet comment, and she knew she'd hit on the truth. Gio's cynicism, his bitterness, had nothing to do with his opinion of her but with the terrible example his own parents had set.

Although the Hamiltons had divorced three years before she and her mum had come to live at the Hall, lurid stories about the split had fed the rumour mill in Hamilton's Cross for years afterwards.

Two impossibly beautiful and volatile people, Claudia Lorenzo, the flamboyant Italian socialite, and Charles Hamilton, the playboy Duke of Connaught, had indulged in years of vicious infighting and public spats, before Claudia had finally stormed out for good, taking their nine-year-old son back to Italy with her. The brutal custody battle that followed had made headlines in both the local and national press. Although Issy had never understood why the Duke had fought so hard for his son when he'd treated Gio so harshly during his court-ordered summer visits.

As a teenager, Issy had found the concept of Gio as a tug-of-love orphan both fabulously dramatic and wonderfully tragic, like something straight out of *Wuthering Heights*, but she could see now it must have been a living hell for him as a child. And could easily have warped his view of relationships ever since.

'Your parents were selfish, self-absorbed people,' she said. 'Who didn't care about love or each other.' *Or you*, she thought. 'But you shouldn't let that make you give up on finding a loving relationship for the rest of your life.'

Gio groaned, dumping his napkin on the table. 'Will you give it a rest? You don't know what you're talking about.'

It wasn't quite the reaction she'd been hoping for, but she wasn't going to give up that easily.

'I know enough,' she countered. 'My mother and I heard how your father shouted at you and belittled you. And I saw for myself how much it upset you,' she persevered, despite the rigid expression on his face. 'On that last night, when I found you in the orchard, you'd just had a massive row with him. You looked so upset. So…' She trailed off as he turned away, a muscle in his jaw twitching. And she realised something she should have figured out years before.

'*That's* why you needed me that night. *That's* why we made love,' she said softly, her heart punching her throat. 'Because of something he said to you.'

His head swung back, his eyes flashing hot, and she knew she'd touched a nerve.

Whatever his father had said that night had made him reach out to someone, anyone, to ease the pain. And, thanks to circumstance, that someone had been her.

The revelation shouldn't really matter now. But it did. She'd believed for ten years that their first night had been a terrible mistake, brought about by her immature romantic fantasies. But what if he really *had* needed her—just not in the way she'd thought?

'We didn't make love,' he said flatly. 'We had sex.'

She didn't even flinch at the crude words. 'What did he say?' she asked, her heart melting at the anguished frown on his face.

'Who the hell cares what he said? That was a million years ago.'

It wasn't a million years ago, but even if it had been it was obvious it still hurt.

'Dammit, you're not going to let this go, are you?'

She shook her head. 'No, I'm not.'

'Fine.' He dumped his napkin on the table. 'He told me I wasn't his son. That Claudia had screwed a dozen other men during their marriage. That I was some other man's bastard.'

Shock reverberated through her body at the ugly words. 'But you must have been devastated,' she murmured. How could the Duke have harboured that nasty little seed in his head all through Gio's childhood? And then told his son? 'But what about the custody battle. Why would he...?'

'He needed an heir.' Gio shrugged. 'And he enjoyed dragging Claudia through the courts, I suspect.'

The words were delivered in a gruff, deliberately contemptuous monotone. But underneath it she could hear a plea that he couldn't quite disguise, of the little boy who had been so easily hurt by the two people who should have cherished him the most.

'Gio, I'm so sorry.' She covered his hand where it lay on the table, and squeezed.

'Why should you be sorry?' he said, pulling his hand out from under hers. 'It didn't matter to me. In fact, it was a relief. I'd always wondered why I could never please the man.'

He was lying. It *had* mattered. He'd brooded for days every time the Duke had reprimanded him as a teenager. She'd seen the hurt and confusion he'd tried so hard to hide behind surly indifference. And she'd seen how unhappy, how volatile he'd been that night.

And still mattered now.

No wonder he found it so hard to believe that love existed. That relationships could last.

His eyes narrowed sharply. 'Bloody hell,' he said. 'Stop that right now.' Standing up he threw a fistful of euro notes on the table.

'Stop what?' she gasped as his fingers locked on her wrist and he hoisted her out of her chair.

'Stop psychoanalysing me.' He shot the clipped words over his shoulder as he walked out of the restaurant, tugging her behind him.

'I'm *not* psychoanalysing you,' she panted, trying to keep up with his long strides. 'I'm just trying to understand why…'

'There's nothing to understand.' He stopped on the street outside, his voice stiff with frustration. 'I wanted you and you wanted me. There wasn't anything significant about that night except you were a virgin. And if I'd figured that out sooner, believe me, I wouldn't have touched you no matter how tempted I was.'

The fervent denial made her emotion swell to impossible proportions. Why did he find it so hard even now to admit he'd needed someone? Even fleetingly?

'All right,' she said placatingly. 'But I still find it moving that—'

'Well, don't.' He cut her off as he marched down the street again. 'Because it's not.' They reached the scooter. 'That night was about animal passion.' Lifting the spare helmet off the handlebars, he thrust it at her. 'Climb aboard, because I've got some more animal passion for you.'

Great. She wasn't feeling that moved any more. 'Stop ordering me about.' She shoved the helmet on her head. Damn, he'd made her pout—and she hated to be a cliché. 'How about if I said I didn't *want* your animal passion?'

'You'd be lying,' he said with infuriating certainty as he mounted the scooter and jammed the key into the ignition. 'Now get on. You've got exactly ten seconds.' He stamped his foot on the start pedal. 'Or we're going to be doing it against the back wall of Latini instead of in the privacy of my bedroom. Your choice.'

'I will *not* get on your scooter!' she shouted, as colour flooded her cheeks at the sensual threat—and her traitorous nipples pebbled beneath the thin silk of her blouse.

'Ten…'

'How dare you talk to me like that?' she cried, flustered now, as well as outraged.

'Nine…'

He's kidding. He has to be.

'Eight…'

'I am not your personal floozy!'

One dark brow arched. 'Seven…'

Her knickers got moist.

'Six…'

'And, frankly, you've got an awfully high—'

'Five…'

'—opinion of your powers of seduction,' she tried to scoff, but rushed the words.

'Four…' He slung his arm across the handlebars of the scooter, looking relaxed but ready—like a tiger waiting to pounce. 'Three…'

'As if you could get me to *do it* with you in a public place,' she hedged desperately, her voice rising. Time was running out.

'Two…' He stood up on the scooter, looming over her.

She slapped her hands on her hips. 'Now, listen here—'

'One.'

Oh, hell.

She scrambled onto the seat behind him and grabbed two fistfuls of his T-shirt.

'All right. All right.' She yanked. 'You win. For now,' she said, sighing with relief as he sank back with a triumphant chuckle.

'I'm so not finished talking about this, though,' she continued, fighting a rearguard action as he revved the engine and she wrapped her arms around his waist. 'You arrogant, oversexed…'

The protest was lost in the roar of the Vespa's engine as it careered away from the kerb.

Issy clung on, her mind spinning, her tender breasts vibrating against the muscled sinews of his back.

As they sped over the Ponte Vecchio she caught sight of a couple embracing in the shadows of the ancient bridge. And agonising desire flooded between her thighs.

She held on for dear life. What were the chances she was going to be in any fit state to conduct a conversation, let alone an argument, once they got back to the villa?

Not a lot, actually.

After the fifteen-minute journey up the hill, Gio clasped her hand in his and walked through the darkened house. He didn't utter a word. And neither did she. Too preoccupied by the thought of the animal passion they had already sampled to remember why she'd objected to sampling some more.

Within seconds of slamming his bedroom door, he had her naked.

As he flung off his own clothing she stood shaking, mesmerised by the hard, masculine beauty of his body gilded in the moonlight. Then her eyes snagged on the powerful erection jutting out as he sheathed himself.

And the animal passion that had smouldered all evening leapt into flame.

'No more delaying tactics.' He lifted her easily in his arms. 'There's nothing to understand.' Gripping her thighs, he hooked her legs around his waist. 'All we need is this.'

'Why can't we do both?' she asked, as her back

thudded against the door. But she knew she was fighting a losing battle as the head of his erection probed at the folds of her sex.

His eyes met hers in the half-light. 'Later, Isadora.' He planted a possessive kiss on her lips. 'We're busy.' And impaled her in one powerful thrust.

She sobbed at the fullness of the penetration.

Okay, later works, she thought vaguely, as he sank in to the hilt.

A long time later, her body aching from an overdose of physical activity and sexual pleasure, they finally collapsed onto his huge *bateau* bed.

'Do you think we'll ever get to slow and easy?' she mumbled, curling against his side and pillowing her head on his shoulder, so tired she would happily beg for oblivion.

She heard his chuckle, felt the soft rumble in his chest before his arm drew her close and his hand caressed her bottom. 'That would be next time. Now, go to sleep.'

Her eyes fluttered closed as his lips brushed her hair, and she heard him take a deep breath before releasing it.

'Issy. What the hell am I going to do with you?' he murmured.

Despite the fuzziness of exhaustion, she heard the confusion in his voice and felt her heart stutter in response.

Become my friend again.

She nestled deeper into his embrace as the warm, languid afterglow of sensational sex pulled her into a dreamy sleep.

CHAPTER SEVEN

'WAKE UP, Sleeping Beauty, you need to get out of the sun before you end up with third degree burns.'

Issy shaded her eyes to see Gio standing by her sun-lounger, looking tall and delicious in chinos and an open-necked shirt.

'You're back already?' She stretched lazily, ignoring the persistent flutter beneath her breastbone at the sight of him. He'd left for a meeting in town after breakfast, and she'd taken a swim in the pool. It was a surprise to see him back so soon.

He crouched down on his haunches until they were eye to eye. 'I've been gone for over two hours.' He rested his arm across his knee and touched her nose. 'And you're looking a little pink.'

'What's the time?' she asked groggily, determined not to read too much into how her spirits lifted at his look of concern.

Despite Gio's assertions that all they had was animal passion, they had drifted into friendship again as easily as breathing. After only a few days the companionship they shared had become as exciting as their sexual relationship.

If the first day's sightseeing had been magical, yesterday's had been even more so. They'd brushed shoulders with businessmen and market traders alike in a *trattoria* at the Mercado Centrale, while Gio had chuckled at her pathetic attempts to order in Italian. He'd taken her to see the stunning golden mosaics in the Romanesque basilica of San Miniato al Monte, then cuddled with her under the stars as they watched *La Dolce Vita* in flickering black and white on the ten-foot open-air screen in a nearby park.

In the last twenty-four hours she'd seen a man emerge who was cultured and charismatic, had a decidedly mischievous sense of humour, and was passionate about his work and the beautiful city he lived in.

Maybe they hadn't talked about their past or anything else too personal again—something she knew was deliberate on Gio's part—but she hadn't pushed. Taking the sweet, steady glide into friendship and getting an enchanting glimpse of what that unhappy boy had made of his life had been enough. Frankly, friendship didn't get much better than this. Why ruin the mood?

Gio glanced at his watch. 'It's after one,' he replied. 'And about the hottest time of the day.'

'Oh.' She'd been asleep for over an hour. And would probably be a bit sore tomorrow as a result. Thank goodness she'd slathered factor fifty sunscreen on before she'd dozed off.

She gave a jaw-breaking yawn and sighed. 'I don't know why you're looking at me like that. This is all your fault.'

'How?'

'You're the one who hasn't let me sleep since I got here,' she teased, although it wasn't far from the truth.

This was a friendship with some exceptional benefits, she thought, as her pulse spiked at the sight of his trousers stretching across muscled thighs.

They'd done hard and fast, slow and easy, and everything in between. Gio's powers of recovery had proved to be Herculean, and she'd never been more satisfied, more sated—or more exhausted—in her life. When she'd woken up snuggled in his arms that morning, inhaling the familiar musk of his scent had sent shockwaves through her oversensitised flesh, but her hunger had been as insistent as ever when his morning erection had brushed her bottom.

Okay, so she'd felt a strange dragging sensation when he'd left her to shower alone this morning because he had an important meeting. But she hadn't let it bother her. The let-down feeling was to be expected. They were having a fabulous time, but it would be over soon. The ennui was probably just to do with endorphins, or something.

'Exactly how long have you been out here?' he asked. 'Did you even put on any cream?'

Her grin widened. 'Yes, boss.'

'It's not funny,' he said, all serious and intense. 'You've got very fair skin. Sunburn's no joke.'

'Spoken by a man who's probably never had it.' She ran her fingernail over one tanned bicep, enjoying the way the muscle bunched. 'Honestly, Gio. You sound like my mum.'

'Oh, yeah?' His eyebrow lifted, the frown replaced by a slow smile.

'Yes, yeah,' she said, desire curling anew in her belly. 'Just for that…'

She shrieked as he thrust one hand under her knees and the other behind her back.

'What are you doing?' she said, gripping his neck as he straightened with her wriggling in his arms.

'Helping you cool off.'

She started to wriggle in earnest when she saw his direction. 'No. No way. I've already had a swim today.' And the water would feel freezing after she'd been lying in the sun.

Ignoring her protests and her struggles, he hefted her towards the pool. 'Yes, but I haven't,' he said, and stepped off the edge fully clothed.

'So, is that sunburn or are you still blushing?' Gio asked, a teasing smile lurking on his lips.

'I don't know what you're talking about.'

He sat at the terrace table, his wavy hair furrowed into slick rows, damp wisps of chest hair visible through the open lapels of his robe.

'I had no idea you could move that fast.' He poured a glass of lemonade from a pitcher on the table and passed it to her. 'I think you may have set a land-speed record.'

She took a swallow of the icy drink to calm the giddy beat of her pulse. 'It's not remotely funny,' she said dryly, trying to control her flush. 'Your housekeeper will think I'm a tart.'

If she doesn't already.

They'd been about to ravage each other during their impromptu dip when Carlotta had interrupted them to announce that lunch had been set out on the terrace. Issy had scurried off to the bedroom wrapped in a towel and dying of embarrassment. Gio's laughter had echoed behind her. She still hadn't quite managed to get over her mortification.

'No, she won't,' he said lazily, slicing into the veal *parmigiana* on his plate. 'She's Italian. They don't get as hung up on social niceties as you Brits.'

'You Brits? Aren't you half-British?'

He grinned. 'When it comes to social niceties, I'd say I'm more Italian.'

'So would I,' she said emphatically.

He chuckled.

Issy smiled back. But as she crossed her legs and smoothed her robe over her knees the heat continued to burn in her cheeks.

How could she not have noticed Carlotta beside the pool?

And how could she have got carried away like that, knowing there was a houseful of servants who could interrupt them at any minute? Gio had turned her from nun to nymphomaniac in the space of a few days—and it was starting to concern her.

Shouldn't the passion have begun to fade a little by now?

Gio lifted her hand off the table and linked his fingers with hers. 'In deference to your British sensibilities, I suggest we retire to the privacy of the bedroom after lunch.'

The familiar thrill shot through her as he pressed his lips to her knuckles. Concerning her even more. Why couldn't she say no to him? Ever?

Carlotta stepped onto the terrace, holding a small silver tray, and Issy tugged her hand free.

Gio took a large envelope off the tray and thanked the housekeeper. Issy sent Carlotta what she hoped was a friendly smile and the woman smiled back, apparently unperturbed by what she'd almost interrupted in the pool.

As Issy watched the housekeeper leave, she wondered how many more of Gio's sexual escapades Carlotta had witnessed. The instant prickle of jealousy made her frown. This was temporary—with no strings attached. Gio's other women didn't matter to her in the least.

'Dammit.'

At the whispered curse, she turned to see Gio dump a large magnolia card into the wastepaper bin and throw the torn envelope on top.

'What was that? It's not bad news, is it?'

'No, it's nothing,' he said as he picked up his knife and fork.

The movement made his robe gape open. Issy pulled her gaze away from the sprinkle of dark hair that arrowed down his abdomen.

It wasn't nothing. That much was obvious from the tense, annoyed expression on his face.

Brushing off the torn envelope, she lifted the card out of the bin. The fancy gold lettering was in Italian, but she could make out today's date.

Why had he reacted so violently to something that looked so innocuous?

'Who is Carlo Nico Lorenzo?' she asked, reading out the name printed in the centre of the card.

He glanced up, his eyes stormy. 'I threw that away for a reason. It's rubbish.'

'Is he a relative of yours?' she asked, pretending she hadn't heard the rude comment as curiosity consumed her. 'Did your mother have brothers and sisters?' She trailed off, waiting for him to fill in the blanks.

'Carlo is the baby they're baptising,' he said curtly, then leaned forward and plucked the invitation out of her hand. 'He's the grandson of Claudia's oldest brother. Who's also called Carlo.' He dumped the card onto the table, face down. 'Now, can we finish our lunch?'

'You mean he's your uncle's grandson?' she prompted. Why had he never mentioned his Italian family before? She'd had no idea he had relatives in Italy.

'I guess.' He bent his head to concentrate on his food. The tactic so deliberate, her curiosity only increased.

Picking up the invitation, she scanned the contents again, then flipped it over. 'What does this say?' She pointed to the spidery handwriting scrawled across the back.

He chewed, swallowed, his eyes narrowing. 'You know, Issy, sometimes your persistence can be very annoying.'

She waited calmly for a proper answer.

He huffed, snatched the card and read aloud. 'It says: "We miss you, Giovanni. You are family. Please come this time."' He flicked the card back into the bin. 'Which is insane, because I hardly know the man—or his family.'

'This time? How many times have they invited you to a family event?' It went without saying that he'd never attended any—had probably never even bothered to RSVP.

'I don't know. Hundreds.' He blew out a frustrated breath. 'There's a lot of them. Claudia had five older brothers, and they all had tons of kids. There's an event every other week.'

'Where do they live?' Maybe they lived on the other side of Italy? Maybe that was why he had never bothered to visit them?

'About an hour's drive,' he said. 'The family owns an olive farm near San Giminiano. Most of them still live around there, I guess.' He sent her a bored look. 'So, do you want to tell me why you're so interested?'

A spurt of temper rose up.

Her own family had only consisted of her and her mother. She'd always dreamed of having more. Of having brothers and sisters, cousins and aunts and uncles. She knew perfectly well Gio was an only child too—and from what he'd already told her she knew he'd been a lot more alone than she had as a child. So why hadn't he embraced the chance to get to know his own family?

'For goodness' sake, Gio,' she said, riding the temper. 'Why haven't you been to see them? They're your *family*.'

'I don't have a family. I don't even know them,' he continued. 'They disowned Claudia before I was even born. Cut her out of their lives.'

'Is that why you dislike them?' she asked, confused now, and a little appalled by his indifference. 'Because they treated your mother badly?'

'Of course not!' He sounded annoyed now—annoyed and something else she couldn't quite define. 'I expect she made their lives a misery. I can testify to the fact that she was a nightmare to live with, so I don't blame them for kicking her out.'

She heard the contempt in his voice. So that was why he never talked about his mother.

'Are you upset that they never got to know you as a boy, then?' Issy asked carefully, still trying to understand his hostility towards the rest of his family. *Why* was he so determined to have nothing to do with them?

He pushed his plate away and reached for the pitcher of lemonade. 'Issy, in case you haven't realised yet—'

he poured himself a glass, gulped some down '—this conversation doesn't interest me.'

'Well, it interests *me*,' she said, determined not to back down—not this time. 'I think you *do* blame them. But you shouldn't. It doesn't—'

'I don't blame them.' He shoved his chair back, walked to the balcony rail. 'Why should they care about me? I'm nothing to them.'

Her temper died as she heard the defensiveness in his tone, saw his knuckles whiten where they gripped the terrace rail.

'That's clearly not true,' she said, feeling desperately sad for him. 'Or why would they have invited you to this christening?' She watched his shoulders tense, but he didn't say anything. 'There must be a reason why they didn't try to get to know you as a child. Maybe they—'

'They did try,' he interrupted her. 'I met Carlo. Once. He came to our apartment in Rome.' He paused, his voice barely audible above the breeze. 'Claudia wasn't there. She'd been out all night at some party, and I was in the place alone.'

'How old were you?' she asked gently. She'd tried not to think of him as a boy too much since their first night in Florence. Had tried not to make the mistake of reading too much into his parents' behaviour and its effect on him. But now she wanted to know. How bad had it been?

'Ten,' he said, as if it weren't particularly significant.

She bit down on her lip, tried not to let the thought of that neglected boy get to her.

But then another shattering thought occurred to her, and she felt tears sting the back of her throat.

As long as she had known Gio he had always called his parents Claudia and the Duke. Even as a boy he had never referred to them as Mum or Dad. And now Issy knew why. Because in all the ways that counted they had never been his mother and father. Just people who had battled over him and then rejected him.

'What happened?' She asked. 'With Carlo?'

Gio shrugged, the movement stiff. 'Not a lot. He asked to see Claudia. We waited together for her to come home. He told me who he was, asked me about myself. How old was I? What did I like doing? My Italian wasn't great then, and his questions confused me.'

He sounded so puzzled, even now, and her heart ached. No wonder Gio had no faith in relationships, in family. He'd never been part of one. Not one where people cared for you and about you and were interested in what you did and said.

'She came home eventually,' he said, derision edging his voice. 'Coked up to the eyeballs as usual. They had a massive row, she called the police, and he had to leave. He never came back. But the invitations started to come a few months later. Always addressed to me. She threw them away—wouldn't let me open them. After her death I replied to a few, giving excuses why I couldn't come, but they didn't get the hint so now I throw them away.'

'I think you should go.' Taking the card back out of the bin, she crossed the balcony, placed a hand on his back. 'I think you should go to this christening. See your family. See Carlo again.' Suddenly it seemed vitally important.

He turned round, stared down at the card she held but didn't take it.

'Issy, for God's sake.' He cupped her cheek in his

palm, his eyes shadowed. 'Haven't you heard a word I've said? I don't want to go. I don't belong there,' he murmured.

She rested her hand on his heart, felt the rapid beats. 'Yes, you do. You don't have to be scared of them, you know.'

'I'm not scared. Don't be idiotic.'

But she could hear defensiveness behind the irritation.

He was scared. He was scared to let them get too close. To trust them. To trust anyone.

Her heart clutched as he looked away.

Every child deserved to be loved unconditionally, supported in whatever they chose to do. She thought of the way her own mother had loved and supported her in every mad decision she'd ever made in her life. Edie had always been there. Praising her as if she'd been Sarah Bernhardt when she'd played a tomato in her first school play. Providing a shoulder to cry on when she'd bawled her eyes out over Gio. Even nagging her into admitting that her lifelong dream of becoming an actress needed some serious tweaking after she'd begun her job at the Crown and Feathers and discovered that she preferred bossing people about to angsting about her motivation.

For all his apparent confidence and charisma, Gio had never had any of that as a child. He'd been entirely alone—criticised and rejected by his father, or neglected and ignored by his mother. Even though he'd made a staggering success of his life, he'd survived emotionally by closing himself off and convincing himself he didn't need love.

He'd persuaded himself it wasn't important, that it didn't matter to him, when obviously it did.

Gio had needed a friend as a boy, and he still needed one now. To show him there was another way.

'They can make your life so much richer, Gio. Can't you see that?'

He gave a harsh laugh. 'You've still got a romantic streak a mile wide, haven't you?' He leaned back against the rail, his stance deliberately casual. 'I'm not interested in meeting Claudia's family. I've got nothing to offer them. And they've got nothing to offer me.'

She stared at him, saw stubborn refusal, but she knew it wasn't true. He had so much to give. And he could get so much back in return.

'There's only one thing I need.' He took the invitation from her. 'And it's got nothing to do with this.' He flicked the card onto the table behind her.

He grasped her waist, tugged her close, then slanted his lips across hers.

She curled her fingers into his hair and kissed him back, not caring that he was trying to make a point. Not caring any more what the point was. Because she could taste his desperation right alongside his desire.

He bracketed her waist, boosted her into his arms. 'Wrap your legs around me.'

She did as he commanded, feathering kisses over his brow, his chin, his cheeks, as he strode through the French doors into the master bedroom.

He took her mouth again as he lay beside her, his hard, beautiful body covering hers. The kiss was so deep and dangerous and full of purpose she wanted to scream.

They wrestled their robes off together.

He delved into the curls at her core with clever, insistent fingers.

'I love the way you're always wet for me,' he murmured as she bucked beneath him, cried out, the twist and bite of arousal so vicious it stunned her.

She peaked in a rush of savage sensation. Before she had a chance to draw a steady breath he gripped her hips and settled between her thighs.

She grasped his shoulders, opened for him as he plunged.

The fullness of the strokes had her building to a crescendo again with staggering speed, the harsh grunts of his breathing matching her broken sobs. But instead of cresting this time she cruised the brutal orgasm for an eternity, shooting up and then clawing back until she felt trapped in a vortex of pleasure too intense to survive.

Straining, desperate, she crashed over into the abyss at last, and heard his roar of fulfilment as he crashed and burned behind her.

Issy combed the damp curls at his nape with shaking fingers, her body still quivering from the aftermath of the titanic orgasm.

Had that been sex? She felt as if she'd just survived an earthquake.

He lifted his head. But he didn't speak. He looked as stunned as she felt. Easing out of her, he flopped down by her side.

Then cursed. 'I didn't wear a condom. Is that going to be a problem?'

The flat words took a moment to penetrate her fuzzy brain. 'Sorry. What?'

'No condom.' He cleared his throat. 'I forgot.' He propped himself up on his elbow, leaned over her. 'When's your next period?'

'I...' She tried to grasp the meaning, the rigid tone.

'You're not in the middle of your cycle, are you?'

'No. No, I'm not. I'm due soon.' She did a quick mental calculation. 'Tomorrow, I think.'

He lay back on the bed. 'Thank God.' The relief in his voice made her cheeks burn.

'What about emergency contraception?' she whispered, her mind trying to cling to practicalities. 'Is there somewhere near here we could get it?' The thought of taking the morning-after pill, something she'd never had to do before, made her stomach clench.

'You'd probably need a prescription,' he said, so matter-of-factly it made her heart pound.

'Oh.' She sat up, disorientated. 'It doesn't matter. It'll probably be fine,' she said, the words catching in her throat. 'I can get it from a pharmacy in the UK—perhaps I should arrange a flight just in case.' They hadn't talked about when she would leave. Why hadn't they talked about it? It suddenly seemed vitally important. 'I'll look into that now.' She swung her feet off the bed, struggling for calm as she pulled on her robe.

He caught her arm as she tried to stand. 'You're being irrational. There's no need to book a flight.' He paused. 'I'll get the jet to take you.' He caressed the inside of her elbow with his thumb. 'But let's wait till tomorrow.'

The quiet comment brought with it a rush of excitement that made no sense at all.

This was silly. She should leave—sooner rather than later after their little accident—so why was she so pleased with the casual offer?

'But we only agreed to a couple of days.' She should go. Why didn't she want to?

He brushed her hair behind her ear. 'We did something stupid, that's all. You said yourself it probably won't lead to anything.' He tucked his index finger under her chin.

She tried to rein in her galloping heartbeat. His eyes were full of an intensity she'd never seen before.

'Don't worry. We'll sort it out if we need do.' His deep, steady voice was reassuring, the stroke of his hand on her hair making her heart-rate slow to a canter.

Why did it feel as if everything had spun off its axis and nothing made any sense any more?

He took her shoulders, held her at arm's length to look into her eyes. 'Let's not think about it today. Tomorrow is soon enough. Go and get dressed. Wear something fancy. We'll go somewhere special.' He brushed a kiss across her brow, making her smile despite her confusion. 'It'll take our minds off it.'

'Do you really think—'

'We can go anywhere you want,' he interrupted her. 'Your choice.'

'Okay,' she said, more pleased than she probably should be at the thought that she didn't have to go today.

She hurried into the bathroom, shut the door and leaned back against it, letting the excited little hammer-beats of her pulse drown out the doubts. Everything was fine. More than fine. They'd made a silly mistake, but it didn't have to mean anything.

She'd always found it hard to hold back as a teenager, to weigh and judge and interpret other people's feelings properly. It was the reason she'd fallen so easily for Gio, and she'd worked long and hard in the decade since at keeping her emotions in check and never letting them get the better of her again. But maybe she'd held on too hard, turned herself into someone she really wasn't.

It didn't have to be a bad thing that she had such strong feelings for Gio. They had a shared history, and now she'd spent time with him, and understood the extent of his parents' neglect and what it had done to him, it made sense that she would feel their friendship more keenly.

She twisted the gold-plated taps on the large designer tub.

She'd come here to get over her past mistakes, but surely the best way to do that was to heal the part of herself she'd lost that night. She didn't have to be frightened of her feelings for Gio any more.

When their fling was over they would go their separate ways, having reclaimed the good things from their childhood and left behind the bad.

As the water gushed out, and she sprinkled bath salts, another thought occurred to her and she smiled.

Gio had said she could pick their destination for this afternoon. And she knew exactly where she wanted to go. She wasn't the only one who needed to heal.

But as Issy slipped into the steamy, scented water, and let the lavender bubbles massage her tired muscles, she couldn't quite shake the suspicion she had failed to grasp something vitally important.

* * *

What the hell had he done?

Gio lay on the bed, his arm folded under his head, as he stared at the fan on the ceiling.

He'd taken her without a condom. He turned his head to stare at the bathroom and heard the reassuring hum of running water.

Except he wasn't feeling all that reassured.

Had he totally lost his mind?

He never, ever forgot to wear condoms. Partly for personal safety reasons, but mostly because he had absolutely no desire to father a child. Even if the woman said she was on the pill. No matter how hot he got, or how desperate he was to make love, he always used protection.

But Issy got him hotter and more desperate than any woman he'd ever met—and for the first time ever the thought of contraception hadn't entered his head.

She'd made him feel raw and vulnerable with all that nonsense about getting to know Claudia's family, until he'd been desperate to shut her up. But the minute he'd tasted her, the minute he'd touched her, the usual longing had welled up inside him and all he'd been able to think about was burying himself inside her. Before he knew what was happening he'd been glorying in the exquisite clasp of her body and shooting his seed deep into her womb without a thought to the consequences.

It hadn't been a mistake, or an oversight. It had been sheer madness.

Getting off the bed, he shrugged into his robe, then scraped his fingers through his hair.

How the hell had this happened? He felt more out of control than ever now.

What if she actually got pregnant? He knew Issy. She

would never consider an abortion. But he didn't want a child. He knew what it was like to be an afterthought, an inconvenience, a mistake.

And why had he asked her to stay? By rights he should have been breaking the speed limit to race her to the airport even now, and then piloting the plane back to England to make sure she got whatever she needed to ensure there was no chance of a baby.

Temporary insanity had to be the answer. He slumped into a chair by the terrace table and frowned at the remnants of their aborted lunch. Although he wasn't sure how temporary it was any more.

The woman was driving him nuts. In the last few days he'd become addicted to everything about her.

The fresh, sweet scent of her hair when he woke up beside her in the morning, the sound of her voice as she chatted away about everything and nothing, even the stubborn tilt of her chin and the compassion in those deep blue eyes when she had tried to insist he go to that stupid Christening.

He'd become so enthralled he'd gone to the office this morning just to prove he could. But the plan had backfired—because he hadn't been able to stay away. And then he'd found her on the sun-lounger, her skin pink from too much sun, and he hadn't been able to keep his hands off her.

They'd nearly made a spectacle of themselves in front of Carlotta. And, while he'd found Issy's outraged dignity amusing at the time, it didn't seem all that funny any more.

But the worst moment had come when she'd announced she was going to book a flight home. He'd actually felt his stomach tighten with dread. And it had taken a major effort not to let the panic show.

He never got worked up about women. But he'd got worked up about her.

He walked towards the guest suite, steadfastly resisting the urge to join Issy in the master bath. He needed to take a break, because ravaging Issy senseless wasn't turning out to be the cure-all he'd been hoping for.

He frowned as he entered the bathroom of the guest suite.

Maybe that was the problem. He wasn't used to sharing his home with the women he dated, having unlimited sex on tap. As soon as the novelty wore off he'd be able to let Issy go with no trouble at all. And everything would be back to normal. Getting her out of his system was just taking longer than originally planned.

He reached for the shower control. A trip into town might be just what he needed.

He never would have believed it, but maybe you really could have too much of a good thing.

'You want to go *where*?' Gio's fingers clenched on the Ferrari's steering wheel as all his positive feelings about their afternoon out crashed and burned.

'I have the address right here.'

He watched, stunned into silence, as Issy pulled the christening invitation out of her handbag and reeled off the address.

'You were right,' she chirped. 'It is in San Giminiano. And I've got my posh frock on, just like you suggested. So we're all set.' She smiled, looking deceptively sweet as she pressed the button on the dash to bring up the car's inbuilt navigation system. 'Shall I programme the GPS?'

He shoved the panel back into the dash. 'We've already had this conversation. We're not going,' he said firmly, prepared to argue the point if she decided to sulk.

But instead of the expected pout she simply stared at him. 'You said I could choose. I choose to go to your cousin's christening.'

There was that stubborn little chin again. And it wasn't enchanting him any more.

'He's *not* my cousin.' Why couldn't she get that through her head? 'He's nothing to me. None of them are.'

'If that's the case, why are you so frightened of paying them a visit?'

'I'm *not* frightened.' She'd accused him of that before, and it was starting to annoy him.

'Then prove it,' she said softly.

He opened his mouth to tell her to go to hell. He wasn't ten any more, and he didn't take dares. But then he saw the sympathy, the understanding in her eyes, and the words wouldn't come.

He cursed under his breath. 'Okay, we'll go to the christening.' He flipped up the GPS. 'But you're going to be bored out of your brain. I guarantee it.'

As he stabbed in the co-ordinates, she leaned across the console and kissed his cheek.

'No, I won't be. And neither will you.' Her fingers touched his thigh, stroked reassuringly. 'It's going to be an experience you'll never forget.'

I know, he thought grimly, as he gunned the engine.

CHAPTER EIGHT

'*GIOVANNI, mio ragazzo. Benvenuto alla famiglia.*'

Issy blinked away tears, hearing the gruff affection in the elderly man's voice as he threw his arms wide to greet his long-lost nephew.

Stiff and hesitant in the designer suit he'd worn for a different occasion entirely, Gio leant down and accepted the kisses Carlo Lorenzo placed on his cheeks. The old man chuckled, then clasped Gio's hand with gnarled fingers, talking all the time. Issy hadn't a clue what was being said, but she could guess from the confusion on Gio's face and his short, monosyllabic answers that Carlo was as overjoyed to see him as the rest of his family.

She huffed out a breath, so relieved she had to reach into her purse and find a tissue.

As the Ferrari had swung round the twisting mountain roads to the Lorenzo farm, she'd begun to doubt her decision to make Gio come to the christening.

What if she'd been wrong to suggest he come? What if the family didn't welcome him as she expected?

With each mile that passed Gio had become more tense and withdrawn, answering her questions in curt sentences and handling the car with none of his usual skill. It was the first time she'd ever seen him nervous, and his reaction had forced her into admitting an unpleasant truth.

What had made her think she had the right to meddle in his life? He'd never shown any interest in meddling in hers. They'd been in an intimate relationship for a grand total of three days. An intimate relationship that would be over very soon. Yes, they were friends, but that was all they were. Did that really give her the right to make assumptions about what he needed in his life?

Now, as Carlo continued to chat away to Gio, she let her pleasure at the wonderful way Gio's family had greeted him push the doubts away. This could have gone so horribly wrong. But it hadn't—which counted for a lot.

'You are Giovanni's *ragazza*, yes?'

Issy glanced round to see a petite, pretty and heavily pregnant young woman dressed in a colourful summer dress smiling at her.

Issy stuffed the tissue back into her bag and held out her hand. 'I'm Issy Helligan,' she said quickly, not quite sure how to reply to the question.

Didn't *ragazza* mean girlfriend? Was she Gio's girlfriend? Not really. Not in any permanent sense.

'I'm a friend of Gio's,' she said, feeling oddly dispirited. 'I'm so sorry, but I don't speak much Italian.'

'It is good I speak excellent English, then,' the woman said, her brown eyes—which were the exact shade of Gio's—alight with mischief. 'Or we would not be able to gossip about my long-lost cousin. My name is ——after La Loren.' She wrinkled her nose. 'Sadly, I only got her name and not her body.'

Issy laughed, liking Sophia instantly. 'When is your baby due?' she asked.

Sophia looked down at her bump, her eyes glowing as she stroked it. 'In two weeks. But my husband Aldo says it will be sooner. Our two boys were early, and he will not let me forget it.'

'That's sweet,' she said unable to deny the whisper of envy.

Hearing the love and contentment in Sophia's voice made Issy want to reach for her tissue again. This woman looked younger than her, and she already had two children and another on the way—and a man who loved her.

What on earth have I been doing with my life?

'Come.' Sophia deftly linked her arm with Issy's. 'I have been told to fetch you by my sisters, my aunts and all my girl cousins.' She drew her away from Gio, who looked shell-shocked and a little hunted as Carlo introduced him to more relatives he had never met.

'They all want to know about you and Giovanni,' Sophia added, dropping her voice to a conspiratorial whisper. 'He is like the prodigal son, no? You are very beautiful.' She gave Issy an appreciative once-over. 'And we are very nosy.'

'Oh, Gio and I aren't really…' Issy hesitated. 'We're not exactly…' She paused again. She didn't want to mislead Sophia, but how did she describe what she and Gio were, exactly? 'There isn't that much to gossip about,' she said lamely, glancing over her shoulder. 'And I feel like a traitor leaving Gio alone. I'm the one who suggested he come today.'

Gio glared at her as he was kissed and hugged by a group of older men she assumed were his other uncles.

'Giovanni is a big boy,' Sophia said, patting Issy's arm and tugging her towards a huge trestle table on the farm's flagstone terrace, laden with an array of mouth-watering dishes. 'And he will not be alone.'

A large group of women and girls, ranging in age from twelve to ninety, clustered around the table, watching Issy with undisguised curiosity—making her feel like even more of a fraud.

'My father has been waiting for over twenty years to see *il ragazzo perduto* again,' Sophia added. 'He will be showing him off for hours. But when the dancing starts we will get him back for you.'

Dancing? Issy smiled at the thought. Funny to think she'd never danced with Gio before.

She allowed Sophia to lead her away, ignoring the panicked plea in Gio's eyes. It would do him good to be fêted by his family. That was exactly why they were here. So that he could reconnect with what really mattered in life. And it wouldn't do her any harm to stay out of his way. To absorb the wonder of this large, happy and loving family—and reconnect with her own priorities in life.

'What does *il ragazzo perduto* mean?' she asked absently.

Sophia sent her a warm smile. 'Carlo calls Giovanni "the lost boy". He has worried about him ever since he went to Rome years ago and met him. Carlo said without the family he had no one to love him, to care for him.' Sophia's smile turned knowing. 'But, seeing the way you look at him, I don't think he's lost any more.'

Issy's pulse jumped at the softly spoken words. *Pardon me?*

* * *

'Let's dance, Isadora.'

Issy's head turned at the deep, commanding voice as strong fingers gripped her elbow. 'Oh, hi, Gio.' Her lips tilted up in an instant smile.

He looked confused, harassed and exhausted.

'So you finally escaped from your uncle?' she said brightly.

'Don't you dare laugh.' He skewered her with a quelling look. 'The man has been talking my ear off for two solid hours. And he's introduced me to more people in one afternoon than I've met in my entire life. All of whom he insists I'm related to.'

He treated Sophia and the other women to a quick greeting in Italian, but before any of them could reply, he clamped his hand round Issy's arm and directed her towards the wooden dance floor that had been constructed in the middle of the olive grove.

Dusk was falling, but fairy lights had been hung from the heavily burdened olive trees, casting a magical glow on the couples already slow-dancing in the twilight.

'I've had my cheek pinched by not one but two grannies,' he continued, his voice pained as they stepped onto the uneven boards and he swung her into his arms. 'I've been made to recite my life story about twenty times.' He wrapped his arm round her waist and pulled her flush against his lean, hard body. 'I've been force-fed my Aunt Donatella's *fusilli ortolana* and my second cousin Elisabetta's rabbit *cacciatore*.' He twirled her round in time to the slow, seductive beat of the music before holding her close in his arms. 'And come within a hair's breadth of getting peed on by the guest of honour.'

Issy stifled a laugh as her heart kicked in her chest.

Beneath the confusion and the fatigue she could see the creases around his eyes crinkling and hear the amusement in his voice.

The day had been a success. He looked tired, but happy.

She rested her cheek on his chest, gripped his hand. There had been no need to panic. All the questions she'd been fielding from Sophia and her family had unsettled her, but coming to the christening had been an unqualified success.

'I'm shattered,' he said, leaning down to whisper in her ear, his hands flattening on the bare skin of her back. 'And the only thing that's kept me going is the thought of all the ways I'm going to make you pay for this later tonight.'

Issy pulled away to lay a palm on his cheek. 'Poor Gio. It's tough being loved, isn't it?'

He stopped in the middle of the dance floor. 'What did you say?' His face was masked by the lights behind him, but she could hear his wariness, his sharpness.

'I said it's tough being loved,' she said, wishing she hadn't seen him tense. The emotional stability she'd been working so hard on in the last few hours started to wobble again.

'They don't love me. They're just good people doing what they consider to be their duty.'

They did love him. How could he not see it?

She wanted to argue the point, but knew from the rigid line of his jaw he would refuse to believe it. The ripple of disappointment had her shivering, despite the sultry evening air.

'My father wants me to translate for him.' Sophia stood beside Carlo as the old man clasped Issy's hands.

'Because Giovanni has told him your Italian is not so good. Yet.'

'Oh, has he now?' Issy joked, although her emotions felt perilously close to the surface.

Sophia smiled back as Carlo began to speak in a sober, steady voice, before lifting Issy's hand to his lips and giving it a chivalrous kiss.

Sophia translated. 'My father says that his heart is full with gratitude to you for making Giovanni come today, after being lost to his family for so many years. He says that you are a beautiful woman both inside and out and he hopes that Giovanni can see this too.'

Issy felt herself blush, dismayed by the old man's words.

Carlo turned to Gio and took his hand. Issy felt Gio tense beside her as his uncle spoke. He dipped his head, spots of colour rising on his cheeks beneath his tan as Carlo patted his cheek, his voice rough with pride.

Tears pricked the back of Issy's eyes as Sophia translated.

'My father says that the Lorenzo family is very proud of Giovanni.' Even Sophia's voice sounded more sober than Issy had ever heard it before. 'For all he has made of his life, despite a mother who did not know how to be a mother. Carlo says that Giovanni has made strong, important and beautiful buildings that will stand for a long time.' Sophia swallowed, her voice as thick with emotion as Issy felt. 'But he must not forget that the only thing that lasts forever is a man's family.' Sophia gave a half-laugh as Carlo finished his speech. 'And that Giovanni is getting older and shouldn't waste any more time getting started.'

Issy laughed too, at the old man's audacity and the

roguish sparkle in his eyes. As Gio replied in Italian Issy noticed the measured tone, devoid of his usual cynicism, and felt her heart lift. He wasn't completely blind to what these people had to offer, whatever he might think.

As they said their goodbyes to everyone, Issy's hand strayed automatically to her belly.

What if their mistake ended in a pregnancy?

To her surprise, the question didn't bring the panic she might have expected. But she forced the thought away anyway. A pregnancy was highly unlikely. And today had been quite emotional enough already.

The last to say her goodbyes was Sophia, who gave Issy a final hug as Gio climbed into the Ferrari.

'You must both come to the next *battesimo*, as it will be for my baby,' she whispered, before standing back and winking at Issy. 'And if Giovanni does as he is told, maybe the one after that will be yours.'

Issy waved furiously as Gio reversed the car down the farm track, sniffing back tears and trying not to take Sophia's little joke to heart.

What she and Gio had was fleeting. That had always been understood.

But as the whole family shouted salutations at them, and a group of children raced after the car, a few tears slipped over her lids. This was what it felt like to belong, to be part of something bigger than yourself—and she'd never realised how much she wanted it until now.

'That wasn't so bad,' Gio said, resting his palm on Issy's knee as he turned the car onto the main road.

Issy sank into the leather seat and watched the dark shapes of San Giminiano's fortress walls disappear into the night as Gio accelerated. Leaning her head against the door, she rested her palm on her belly, the emotion of the day overwhelming her.

'Will you go back again?' she asked.

He said nothing for several seconds. 'I doubt it.'

Despite the murmured reply, a tiny smile touched the corners of Issy's mouth. Was it wishful thinking, or did he sound less sure of himself than usual?

Easing up the handbrake, Gio stared at the woman fast asleep beside him in the car. She'd been incredible today. So beautiful, so captivating and so important to his peace of mind. He'd needed her there in a way he never would have anticipated.

All through the afternoon and evening, whenever the impact of being introduced to his family had become too much, his gaze had instinctively searched her out. As soon as he'd spotted her—chatting to Sophia and the other women, or playing games with some of the younger children, or charming his elderly uncles with her faltering Italian—and their eyes connected, his heartbeat had levelled out and the strangling feeling of panic and confusion had started to ease.

At one point she'd been cradling baby Carlo in her arms. He'd marvelled at how she could look so relaxed and happy, as if she were a part of this family, even though these people were strangers and she didn't even speak their language. When his uncle had whispered in his ear, 'She will make an excellent mother for your children, Giovanni. She is a natural.'

The old man was hopelessly traditional and senti-mental. It hadn't taken Gio long to realise that. But the foolish words had still made Gio's heartbeat pound, just as it was doing now.

He continued to stare at her in the moonlight—her rich red hair framing that pale heart-shaped face and her hand lying curled over her belly. A picture of her lush body heavily pregnant with his baby formed in his mind. He imagined her full breasts swollen with milk, the nipples large and distended, and her belly round and ripe, ready to give birth. Desire surged to life so fast he had to grit his teeth.

Okay, this was more than temporary insanity. This was becoming an obsession. An obsession he was beginning to fear he had no control over whatsoever.

Adjusting his trousers, he waited in the darkness until he'd finally calmed down enough to scoop Issy up and carry her to their bedroom without causing himself an injury. She barely stirred. But as he undressed her and tucked her into bed the visions of her body ripe with his child refused to go away.

It wasn't the desire that bothered him, though, as he climbed into bed beside her. Their livewire sexual attraction had always been as natural as breathing. It stood to reason a pregnant Issy would turn him on too.

What disturbed him much more was the irrational need and the bone-deep longing that went right along with the lust.

Sweat trickled down his back as the fear he'd been holding onto with an iron grip all day kicked him in the gut.

Issy squinted at the pre-dawn light filtering through the terrace doors, then moaned softly as cramping pain gripped her abdomen. Gio's warm hand stirred against her hip as she listened to the low murmur of his breathing, and tears caught in her throat. The familiar pain could mean only one thing. She was about to start her period.

She bit down hard on her bottom lip, lifting his hand and laying it down behind her. She didn't want to wake him up and have him see her in this state. Slipping out of bed, she made a beeline for the bathroom.

After taking care of the practicalities, she donned one of Gio's bathrobes and sat on the toilet seat, feeling utterly dejected. Which was ridiculous.

The fact that there was no baby was good news.

She'd have to be an idiot to want to get pregnant under these circumstances. She wasn't ready for motherhood yet. And Gio certainly wasn't ready to be a father. Yesterday's trip had proved that beyond a shadow of a doubt. The man was deeply suspicious of love and families and relationships in general. And even though that may have started to change, it would take a lot more than an afternoon spent with his extended family to repair the damage his parents had done.

But, despite all the calm common-sense justifications running through Issy's mind, she felt as if a boulder were pressing against her chest, making it hard for her to breathe.

She got off the toilet seat and reached for some tissues, swiped at her cheeks to catch the errant tears. She blew her nose, brushed her fingers through her hair and stared blankly into the mirror, but the boulder refused to budge.

As she stared at her reflection she thought of Gio the evening before, his cheeks flushed a dull red while his uncle bade him farewell.

Tenderness and longing and hope surged up. And the boulder cut off her air supply.

'Oh, God!'

She collapsed onto the toilet seat, her fist clutching the tissue, her knees trembling and every last ounce of blood seeping from her face.

'I can't have,' she whispered. 'It's only been a few days.'

But she sank her head into her hands and groaned. Because there was no getting away from it. She'd let her emotions loose and now look what had happened? She'd only gone and fallen hopelessly in love with Giovanni Hamilton. Again.

She wanted to deny it. But suddenly all those wayward emotions made complete sense.

Her Pollyanna-like obsession to get Gio to embrace his family. Her blissful happiness at their renewed friendship. Her relentless attempts to understand the traumas of Gio's childhood and then help him fix them. Even her bizarre anguish at the discovery that she wasn't pregnant.

Her fabulous holiday fling had never been about sex, or friendship, or putting the mistakes of her youth behind her. That had been a smokescreen generated by lust and denial.

She groaned louder.

Fabulous. She may well have just made the biggest mistake of her life. Twice.

It took Issy a good ten minutes to get off the toilet seat. But in that time she'd managed to get one crucial thing into perspective.

Falling in love with Gio again didn't have to be a disaster.

The man she'd come to know wasn't the surly, unhappy boy she'd once fallen for. He was more settled, more content and much more mature now. And so was she.

She hadn't imagined the connection between them in the last few days. The power and passion of their love-making. The intensity of their friendship. Or the aston-ished pride on Gio's face when his uncle Carlo had welcomed him into the bosom of his family.

All of which meant Gio wasn't necessarily a lost cause.

But she also knew that the spectre of that boy was still there. And, given all the casual cruelty that boy had suffered, it wasn't going to be easy for the man to let his guard down and accept that she loved him. Especially not in the space of three days!

After splashing her eyes with cold water, Issy prac-tised a look of delighted relief in the bathroom mirror for when she informed Gio of her unpregnant state.

She mustn't give Gio any clues about how she felt. Not until she'd worked out a strategy. She needed to be calm and measured and responsible this time. The way she *hadn't* been at seventeen. Which meant taking the time to gauge Gio's feelings before she blurted out her own.

Putting her hand on the doorknob, she took a steady-ing breath—and decided not to dwell on the fact that her strategies so far hadn't exactly been a massive success.

Stepping out of the bathroom, she closed the door behind her, grateful for the darkness.

'What's going on? You okay?'

The deep, sleep-roughened voice made her jump.

'Yes. I'm absolutely fine,' she said, forcing what she hoped was a bright smile onto her face.

'You sure?' He paused to rub his eyes. 'You've been in there forever.'

Propped up on the pillows, the sheet draped over his hips, Gio looked so gorgeous she felt the boulder press on her chest again. She made herself cross the room.

'Actually, I'm better than fine. I've got some good news.' She shrugged off the bathrobe and slipped under the sheet. 'I've started my period.'

He frowned, and something flickered in his eyes, but the light was too dim to make it out. 'So you're not pregnant?' he said dully, as his hand settled on her hip, rubbed.

She snuggled into his arms, pressing her back against his chest.

'What a relief, right?' she said, swallowing down the words that wanted to burst out.

Don't say anything, you ninny. It's far too soon.

'Which means there's no need for any emergency contraceptives,' she continued. 'Here or at home. Thank goodness,' she babbled on, the mention of home making the boulder grow. He'd asked her to stay another night. Did that mean he would expect her to leave today?

He said nothing for a long time. His hand absently circling her hip. The only sound was the deafening hum of the air conditioner.

Would he say something? Give her a sign that he'd like her to stay a little longer? She needed more time.

Eventually he moved. Warm palms settled over her belly and stroked gently, easing the ache from the dull cramps.

'That's good,' he said at last, the murmured words devoid of emotion.

Issy placed her hands over his and breathed in his scent. 'Yes, isn't it?' she said, trying to ignore the now enormous boulder.

He hadn't asked her to stay. But he hadn't asked her to leave either. That had to be a good sign. Didn't it?

'*Buongiorno, signorina.*'

Issy blinked at Carlotta's greeting as she pushed herself up in bed, gripping the sheet to cover her nakedness. She pushed her hair out of her eyes and watched the older woman place a tray on the terrace table, put out a plate of pastries, a pot of coffee and one cup.

She felt achy and tired, as if she hadn't slept at all. Probably because she hadn't. All the questions she didn't have answers for had made her emotions veer from euphoria to devastation during the pre-dawn hours as she'd tried to sleep.

'*Scusami, Carlotta. Dové Signor Hamilton?*' she asked, doing her best to pronounce the question correctly.

The housekeeper smiled and replied in Italian, speaking far too fast for Issy to catch more than a few words. Then Carlotta took a folded note out of her apron pocket, passed it to Issy, bobbed a quick curtsy and left.

Issy waited until the door had closed, a feeling of dread settling over her, before glancing at the clock on the mantelpiece. It wasn't even nine o'clock yet. Where could Gio have gone?

She opened the note, her hands trembling. But as she read it her breath gushed out in a shaky puff.

Sorry, Issy.

Had business at the office. You'll have to survive without me today.

Back around dinnertime. Ask Carlotta if you need anything.

Ciao, Gio

A lone tear trickled down her cheek as the hope she'd been clinging to dissolved.

How could he have gone to the office without waiting for her to wake up? She sniffed heavily. Well, she wouldn't have to worry about blurting out her feelings, seeing as he wasn't even here.

It was only after she'd read it three more times that the full import of the curt dismissive note dawned on her.

What had Gio really been hoping for when he'd left this morning? The veiled message in the cursory note seemed obvious all of a sudden. When he returned home tonight, he hoped to discover the sticky business of ending their affair had been dealt with in his absence. He hadn't said anything about her leaving last night because he'd hadn't felt he needed to. It had always been understood that she would go once her period started.

The agony threatened to swamp her as she choked down breakfast and got dressed, but she refused to let any tears fall. There would be time enough for that when she got home.

After breakfast, Issy packed her bag and arranged a flight home via the computer terminal in Gio's study. She rang Maxi and told her she would be at the theatre tomorrow, ready to get back to work. The conversation fortified her. She needed to return to her own life. To start grounding herself in reality again. But as she disconnected the call and keyed in the number Carlotta had given her to book a cab to the airport, her fighting spirit finally put in an appearance.

Her fingers paused on the buttons.

Why was she making this so easy for Gio? Why was she letting him call all the shots, even now?

By keeping quiet about her feelings earlier, by trying to be mature and sensible and take things slowly she'd played right into his hands.

She'd been prepared to give Gio everything—not just her body, but her heart and her soul too. And even if he didn't want them, or the family and the life they could build together, didn't she at least owe it to herself to tell him how she felt?

After getting an address for Gio's office out of Carlotta, Issy booked a cab to take her to the airport. But when the cab arrived twenty minutes later she handed the driver the piece of notepaper with the Florence address scribbled on it, explaining in her faltering Italian that she needed to make a quick stop first.

She had four hours before her flight. More than enough time to see Gio one last time and let him know exactly what he was chucking away.

CHAPTER NINE

EXHAUSTED, but determined, Issy walked into the domed reception area of the stunning glass and steel building on the banks of the Arno.

She'd figured out exactly what she was going to say to Gio and exactly how she was going to say it during the drive into the city. She would be calm, poised and articulate, and would keep a tight grip on her emotions. Under no circumstances would she dissolve into a gibbering wreck as she had at seventeen and let Gio see her utterly destroyed.

Because she wasn't. She'd matured over the last ten years—enough to know that she had to accept the things she couldn't change. However much it hurt. Because she couldn't afford to spend another ten years pining over a man who had nothing to offer her.

'*Mi scusi, parle inglese, signor?*' she asked the perfectly groomed young man at the reception desk, praying he did speak English.

'Yes, signorina. What can I do for you?' he replied in heavily accented English.

'I would like to see Giovanni Hamilton.'

'Do you have an appointment?'

'No, I'm…' She stuttered to a halt, the heat spreading up her neck. 'I'm a friend of his.'

The young man didn't show by a single flicker of his eyelashes what he thought of that statement, but the heat still hit Issy's cheeks as her hard-fought-for composure faltered. How many other women had come to his offices like this? Looking for something he wasn't going to give them?

'I need to see him if at all possible,' she soldiered on. 'It's extremely important.'

To me, at least.

She wasn't sure if the receptionist believed her or simply took pity on her, but he sent her a sympathetic smile as he reached for the phone on his desk. 'I will contact his office manager. What is your name?'

'Isadora Helligan.'

After conducting a brief conversation in Italian, the receptionist hung up the phone.

'His office manager says he is at a site meeting, but if you would like to go up to the top floor she will contact him.'

The stylish young men and women working on state-of-the-art computers and at large drawing easels stopped to watch as Issy walked through the huge open-plan office on the sixth floor—and her composure began to unravel completely.

What was she doing here? Was this another of her hare-brained ideas that was destined to end up kicking her in the teeth? And how the hell was she going to stop herself dissolving into tears with a boulder the size of Mount Everest already lodged in her throat?

Given her tenuous emotional state, she was extremely grateful when Gio's calm, matronly officer manager, who also spoke English, ushered her into Gio's office and informed her that Signor Hamilton had interrupted his meeting at the site office and would be with her in about ten minutes.

Well, at least he wasn't avoiding her.

Unfortunately Gio's office, which took up one whole corner of the floor, was made completely of glass. As she sat down on the green leather sofa adjacent to his desk, and stared out of the floor-to-ceiling window at the Florence cityscape, she could feel the eyes of all his employees burning into the back of her neck.

After suffering from goldfish-in-a-bowl syndrome for an endless five minutes, she paced to the window and stared out at the Florence skyline, the enormity of the task ahead hitting her all over again.

Did she really want to do this? If Gio dismissed her feelings, the way he had done ten years ago, how much harder would it be to pick up the pieces of her shattered heart?

'Issy, this is a nice surprise. Why don't I take you to lunch?'

She lifted her head and saw Gio standing in the office doorway, his shirtsleeves rolled up and his suit trousers creased and flecked with mud. He looked rumpled and ridiculously pleased to see her. His impossibly handsome face relaxed into a sexy, inviting smile.

Mount Everest turned into the Himalayas.

How could she love him so much and not know whether he was even capable of loving her in return?

'I don't have time for lunch,' she said, glad when her

voice hardly faltered. 'I dropped by to tell you I'm catching a flight home this evening.'

The smile disappeared, to be replaced by a sharp frown. He closed the door and walked towards her. 'What the hell for?'

Tell him now. Tell him why.

She tried to find the words, but the dark fury in his eyes shocked her into silence.

'You're not getting a flight home tonight...or to-morrow.' He grasped her arm, hauled her against him. 'You're staying at the villa even if I have to tie you to the bloody bed.'

'You can't do that.' She was so astonished the words came out on a gasp.

'Don't bet on it. This isn't over. And until I decide it is you're not going anywhere. So you'll have to call your people and let them know.'

'My...? What?' she stammered, her mouth drop-ping open.

'*Dio!*' He let go of her arm and stalked past her, a stream of what she assumed were swear-words in Italian coming out of his mouth.

Flinging the door open, he shouted something at a colleague. It was only then that she noticed every one in the office beyond was standing up at their desks and gawking at them. Some were whispering to each other, others were gaping in open curiosity. They'd all heard every word. And, knowing her luck, they probably all spoke perfect English.

But as she stood there being stared at, while Gio's office manager made an announcement to the staff, she simply didn't have it in her to blush. So she and Gio had made a spectacle of themselves? So what? Frankly, she was past embarrassment and past caring what anyone else thought.

She was too busy trying to figure out Gio's temper tantrum.

Clearly he hadn't intended his note to be a thinly veiled invitation for her to go before he got home, as she had suspected.

The news should have pleased her. But it didn't.

Why was he so angry with her? And what right did he have to order her about like that? Had she really been that much of a push-over that he thought he could treat her like his personal possession? This didn't feel like good news. Had they ever really been friends? Or had that been an illusion too?

She waited by the desk, folding her arms across her midriff to stop the tremors racking her body as she watched Gio's employees troop off towards the lifts. Most of them glanced over their shoulders as they left, to get one last juicy look at the crazy lady.

Five long minutes later they were entirely alone, the whole floor having been evacuated.

He propped his butt on the desk, braced his hands on the edge. 'Now, I want to know what's going on.' The stiff tone suggested he was making an effort to keep hold of his temper. 'Why do you want to go home?'

The question had the Himalayas rising up in her throat to choke her. But she couldn't tell him she loved him now. Not until she knew whether she had ever meant more than all the others.

'Why do you want me to stay?'

* * *

I want you to love me.

The plea formed in Gio's mind and he recoiled.

He couldn't say that. Now now. Not ever. He didn't want her love. He didn't want anyone's love.

After lying awake for hours this morning, listening to her sleep, he'd forced himself to leave the house in a desperate attempt to put the whole fiasco out of his head.

Unfortunately burying himself in work hadn't had the effect he'd hoped. Instead of forgetting about her, he'd missed her even more than yesterday. To the point where, when his manager had called to say she'd arrived to see him, he'd broken off an important site meeting to rush back and take her to lunch.

And then she'd told him she was leaving and he'd lost it completely.

He was behaving like a lovesick fool. Which was preposterous. He wasn't in love. He couldn't let himself be in love.

'What do I want?' he replied. 'I want what I've always wanted.' He sank his fingers into her hair, drew her mouth close to his, vindicated by the flash of arousal in her eyes.

Her lips parted instinctively, but as he plundered she dragged her mouth away, staggered back.

'That's not good enough,' she said, the deep blue eyes turbulent with emotion. 'Not any more. I can't stay just for the sex.'

'Why not? It's what we do best,' he said, unable to prevent the bitter edge in his voice.

She'd tricked him into this—just as she'd tricked him into going to that christening yesterday. And now he was paying the price.

She flinched as if he'd struck her. 'Because I want more than that.'

'There isn't any more.'

'Yes, there is. I love you.'

He heard the words, and felt panic strangle him as the great gaping wounds he'd kept closed for so long were ripped open. 'Don't worry, you'll get over it.'

'I don't want to get over it,' Issy stated, the sharp, searing pain at his dismissal ramming into her body like a blow. It had taken every last ounce of her courage to say the words. Only to have them thrown back at her with barely a moment's hesitation.

How could he be so callous? This was worse than the last time—much worse.

'Doesn't it matter to you at all how I feel?' she whispered.

'I told you right from the start I'm not looking for...that.' He couldn't even bring himself to say the word. 'You chose to misinterpret that. Not me.'

She felt numb. Anaesthetised against the pain by shock and disbelief. How could she have been so wrong about him? How could she have been so wrong about everything?

She crossed her arms over her chest, forced her mind to engage. 'I see,' she said dully, her voice on autopilot. 'So this is all my own fault? Is that what you're saying?'

Suddenly it seemed vitally important that she understand. Why had she made so many mistakes where he was concerned?

'Issy, for God's sake.' He stepped close, tried to take

her hand, but she pulled back. 'I never meant to hurt you. I *told* you what I wanted—'

'Why does it always have to be about what *you* want?' she interrupted, allowing resentment through to quell the vicious pain. But as she looked at his handsome face, tense with annoyance, she suddenly understood what it was he had always lacked. And the reality of how he'd played her—of how she'd *let him* play her—became clear.

'I never realised what a coward you are,' she said softly.

He stiffened as if she had slapped him. 'What the hell does that mean?'

She scrubbed the tears off her cheeks with an impatient fist. 'You say all you want is sex, that relationships don't matter to you, because you're too scared to want more.'

'That's insane!' he shouted. But his angry words couldn't hurt her any more.

He'd never wanted what she had to offer—and that was something she would have to learn to live with. But he hadn't needed to be so cruel.

They *had* been friends. She hadn't imagined that. And maybe one day they could have had more—but he'd thrown it away because he didn't have the guts to try. And she knew why.

'Your parents hurt you, Gio. They treated you like a commodity and never gave you the love you deserved. You survived. But you'll never be truly free until you stop letting what they did rule your life.'

'This has nothing to do with them,' he snapped, with the same closed-off expression on his face she had seen so many times before. He still didn't get it—but, worse than that, she knew now he never would.

'Doesn't it?' she said wearily as she walked past him towards the door.

'Come back here, dammit.'

She didn't turn at the shouted words. Didn't have the strength to argue. What would be the point when she could never win?

'I'm not going to come chasing after you, Issy, if that's what all this is supposed to achieve.'

She carried on walking, her heart breaking all over again at the defiant tone.

She had never been the enemy. Why couldn't he see that?

CHAPTER TEN

'DO YOU think our new sponsor will want his company's name on the cover page?'

Issy's fingers paused on the computer keyboard at Maxi's enquiry. 'Sorry? What?' she asked, even though she'd heard every word.

'I'm putting the finishing touches to the new programmes. Shouldn't we add your Duke's company name to it?'

'Yes, I suppose so,' she replied, as the all-too-familiar vice tightened across her torso. 'That's a great idea,' she added, with an enthusiasm she didn't feel.

She'd left Florence over two weeks ago. And she couldn't even talk about the sponsorship without falling apart.

When was she going to get over this?

She didn't want to think about it any more, go on replaying every little nuance of Gio's behaviour during the hours she had spent in his house. Apart from the fact that it was exhausting her, it wasn't going to change a thing.

She'd thought she'd made a major breakthrough a week ago, when she'd come to the conclusion that she hadn't been crazy enough to fall in love after only three short days. She knew now she'd never stopped loving him. In all the years they'd been apart her love had lurked in some small corner of her heart, just waiting to be rediscovered.

But now she knew how hopeless it was, shouldn't she be able to move on?

To start rebuilding her life?

Gio would have moved on the minute she'd walked out the door. And, however sad that made her, she should be grateful. At least his indifference meant his company hadn't pulled the theatre's sponsorship.

She'd allowed herself to get so wrapped up in Gio she'd completely forgotten about the theatre. Which had added a nice thick layer of guilt to the heartache and recriminations in the weeks since her return.

Taking a professional attitude now was essential. And if she had to deal with Gio in the future, as a result of his donation, it would be a small penance to pay. The theatre was now her number one priority.

'Why don't you give the Florence office a call and see what they say?' she said to Maxi, not quite ready to take the next step.

'Are you sure you don't want to ring them?' Maxi asked, a quick grin tugging at her lips. 'They might put you through to the Dishy Duke.'

'No, that's okay,' she said tightly. 'I'm busy doing Jake's bio.' She turned back to her keyboard.

She hadn't told Maxi what had happened in Florence, despite a lot of probing, and she didn't intend to. Talking about it would only make it harder to forget.

She continued to type, glad when the hammer thumps of the keys shut out Maxi's call to Florence. But as she tapped in the final piece of biographical information from Jake's scribbled notes she couldn't miss the sound of Maxi putting the phone back in its cradle.

'Everything go okay?' Issy asked, as casually as she could.

'Better than okay,' Maxi said excitedly. 'Thank God I happened to call them. The e-mail must have got lost.'

'What e-mail?' Issy asked, a strange sinking feeling tugging at the pit of her stomach.

'The e-mail informing us about his visit.' Maxi glanced at her watch. 'His plane touched down over an hour ago, according to his PA. He could be here in less than an hour.' Springing up, Maxi began stacking the files on her desk. 'We should get this place cleared up. I expect he'll want to come up here and check out the office before he catches the afternoon show.'

The sinking feeling turned to full-on nausea. All her erogenous zones melted and a vicious chill rippled down her spine.

'Who are you talking about?' Issy asked, but her voice seemed to be coming from a million miles away. All her carefully constructed walls were tumbling down, to expose the still battered heart beneath.

'The Dishy Duke,' Maxi said confidently. 'Who else?'

'When did you say she'd be back?' Gio lifted the ale glass to his lips, but the lukewarm beer did nothing to ease the dryness in his throat as he glanced round the mostly empty pub.

He noticed the autographed photos on the wall, the yellowing playbills under glass. Issy had talked about this place often during their time together in Florence.

But had he ever really listened, or even bothered to ask her about it? While her assistant had showed him round this afternoon, and he'd been introduced to all the people who worked here and clearly adored Issy, he'd come to realise how much work she'd put into the place and how much it meant to her—and yet he'd been too self-absorbed, too wrapped up in his own fears to notice.

He'd been a selfish bastard about that, as well as about everything else. How could he even begin to make amends?

Issy's assistant sent him a puzzled look, probably because he'd asked her the same damn question approximately fifty times since he'd arrived at the tiny theatre pub two hours ago.

'I'm really not sure. Would you like me to try her mobile again?' she replied, polite enough not to mention that she'd given him the same answer ten minutes ago.

He put his glass down on the counter.

How the hell had Issy got word of his arrival? He'd been careful not to tell anyone but his PA of his plans, just in case she did a vanishing act.

He stared at the girl, who was looking at him with a helpful smile on her face. He couldn't wait any longer. Which meant he'd have to throw himself on this girl's mercy.

It made him feel foolish, but any humiliation was likely to be minor compared to what he would face when he finally got Issy alone again.

Don't go there.

He forced the panic back. That was exactly what had got him into this mess in the first place.

'I need to ask you a favour,' he said, hoping he didn't

sound as desperate as he felt. If she said no, he'd have to find out where Issy lived, which could cost him another night. Now he'd finally built up the courage to do this thing, he needed to get on with it.

The girl's eyebrows lifted. 'Of course, Your Grace.'

'Call me Gio,' he said, straining for the easy charm which had once come so effortlessly. 'I didn't come here to see the theatre. I came to see Issy.'

The girl didn't say anything, her eyes widening.

'We had a disagreement in Florence.' Which was probably the understatement of the millennium. 'I think she's avoiding me.'

'Oh?' the girl said. 'What's the favour?'

'Call her and tell her I've left. I can wait in your office until she gets back, and then say what I need to say.' Although he didn't have a clue what that was yet.

The girl stared at him.

The murmured conversation of the pub-goers got louder, more raucous, and the musty smell of old wood and stale beer more cloying as he waited for the girl's answer.

How had he managed to screw things up so badly?

Ever since he'd returned home from the office that day he'd known he'd made a terrible mistake. But he had refused to admit it.

Anger had come first. Just as it had all those years before. He'd spent a week furious with Issy. How *dared* she delve into his psyche and tell him what he'd made of his life wasn't enough? He'd thrown himself back into work. Determined to prove it was all he needed.

But as the days had dragged into a week the anger had faded, leaving a crushing, unavoidable loneliness in its wake. She'd been at the house for only a few short days—how could he miss her so much?

He'd tried to persuade himself the yearning was purely sexual. And the mammoth erections he woke up with every single morning seemed like pretty good proof. But even he had to accept, as the days had crawled past and the yearning had only got worse, that this was more than just sex.

Whenever he had breakfast he imagined her smiling at him across the terrace table, and felt the loss. Whenever he woke up in the night he reached for her instinctively, but she was never there. He couldn't even visit any of the galleries and churches he loved, because without her there he couldn't see the beauty any more. But what he missed most was the simple pleasure of listening to her talk. The silence had become acute, like a suffocating cell that followed him about, just as it had during his childhood, before he'd met her.

He'd been sitting in his office that morning when he'd finally acknowledged the truth. The only way to remedy the problem was to get Issy back.

He didn't kid himself it would be easy. But he had to try.

He studied her assistant, trying to hold on to his patience. What was taking the girl so long?

Finally she pulled her mobile out of her pocket, began keying in a number. As she lifted it to her ear she sent him an astute look. The helpful smile had vanished.

'Just so you know, I don't care if you are a duke. Or if you're the theatre's angel. If you hurt her, I'll have to kill you.'

He nodded, knowing the reckless threat wasn't the worst that could happen.

'Is Maxi still here?' Issy shouted above the pub crowd to Gerard, one of the barmen.

'Think she's backstage,' he replied, pulling a pint of Guinness. 'Dave had a wardrobe emergency with one of the trolls. I can send Magda to get her.'

'No, that's okay.' She was being ridiculous. Maxi had told her over an hour ago that Gio had left. She needed to stop being such a wuss.

Dipping behind the bar, she sent Gerard a quick wave and started up the narrow staircase to the office. It was after seven, and she still had all the ticket sales from the matinee and evening shows to put on the computer and bank. Staying away all afternoon meant she was going to be here till gone midnight, finishing up, but she didn't care as she pushed open the door. Maybe she'd be able to face Gio again one day, but why pile on the agony before she was ready?

'Hello, Isadora.'

She whipped round at the husky words, her heart ramming full-pelt into her ribcage.

He sat at her desk, looking exactly like the man who had haunted her dreams. One leg was slung over his knee, his hand gripping his ankle, and his hair was combed back from his brow.

She turned back to the door. Staccato footsteps stamped on the wooden floor as her frantic fingers slipped on the knob. She dragged the door open but a large hand slapped against the wood above her head and slammed it closed.

His big body surrounded her as she continued to struggle pointlessly with the handle. She breathed in the spicy scent of his aftershave and her panic increased to fever pitch. The ripple of sensation tightening her nipples and making her sex ache.

'Don't run away, Issy. We need to talk.'

Hot breath feathered her earlobe. They had been in the same position all those weeks ago at the club. Her response to his nearness had been just as immediate, just as devastating then. But why couldn't her body be immune to him even now?

'I don't want to talk,' she said, her voice shaking with delayed reaction. 'Leave me alone.' Her knees buckled.

His arm banded around her midriff, held her upright. 'Are you okay?'

She shook her head. His prominent arousal evident even through their clothes. She tried to pry his arm loose. She couldn't afford to fall under his sensual spell again.

'If you've come here to have sex, I'm not interested,' she said, the melting sensation at her core making her a liar.

'Ignore it,' he said as he let her go, stepped back. 'I came to talk, Issy. Nothing else. I don't have any control over my body's reaction to you.'

She forced herself to face him. 'Once you've said what you have to say, do you promise to leave?'

Regret flickered in his eyes, and his jaw tensed, but he nodded. 'If that's what you want.'

She edged away from the door, moved to stand behind her desk, needing the barrier between them. 'Go on, then,' she prompted.

He said nothing for what seemed like an eternity. The only sound was the muffled noise from the pub downstairs.

'I want you back.'

The irony struck her first. A few short weeks ago she would have given anything to hear him say that. But then anger seeped in. How pathetic. To think she would have settled for so little. 'What do you expect me to say to that?'

He ducked his head, sank his hands into his pockets. When he lifted his head she saw something she hadn't expected. 'I want you to say you'll give me another chance.'

It almost made her weaken. The plea in his voice, the look of raw need darkening the chocolate brown. But she knew she couldn't give in—not after everything he'd put her through.

'I can't.' She pressed her lips together, swallowed the ball of misery back down. 'I've already given you too many chances. I've loved you ever since we were kids. I don't want to love you any more.'

He stepped forward, braced his hands against the desk. 'That's not true,' he countered. 'You didn't love me when you were a girl. That was infatuation.'

'No, it wasn't,' she cried, temper strengthening her voice. How could he ask her for another chance and still belittle her feelings?

'You fooled yourself into believing it, Issy. Because you were young. And sweet.' He turned away.

She shook her head. 'That's not true. I was immature. I know in many ways I was still a child. But I did love you. Because when I met you again the feelings were all still there.'

He swung back. 'No, they weren't. You detested me,' he said. 'You said so yourself.'

Despite the off-hand remark she could see the anguish in his eyes, and she realised the rash words had hurt him.

She'd assumed he couldn't be hurt, that she had never meant that much to him. But what if she had misjudged the strength of his feelings all along? In the same way as she'd misjudged her own.

'Why did you push me away?' she asked, tentative hope flickering to life. 'Why didn't you believe me when I said I loved you?'

He gave a deep sigh. 'You're going to make me say it, aren't you?'

She heard the turmoil, the resignation in his voice, and hope blossomed. 'Yes, I am.'

His eyes met hers. 'Because I'm not the man you think I am.'

'And what man is that?' she asked simply.

He dipped his head, the gesture weary. 'One that deserves you.' His voice broke on the words and she realised that finally, after all these years, all the heartache and confusion, the barriers were at last crumbling away.

'Gio, you idiot,' she murmured. 'What makes you think you don't deserve me?'

'I spent my whole childhood trying to make them care about me. And they never did. I knew there had to be a reason. Then you came along and filled up all those empty spaces. And I never even had to ask.'

'But you kept shutting me out.' He'd done the same thing when they were children, as soon as she'd got too close. 'Why would you do that?'

'Because I was petrified,' he murmured. 'I didn't

want to need you and then have you figure out you'd made a mistake.'

Stepping out from the desk, she wrapped her arms round his waist, laid her head on his chest. And the last of the chill burned away as his hands settled on her shoulders.

'You were right, Issy. I've let what they did control my life. I'm not doing that any more.' His lips brushed her hair. 'Give me another chance. I know you probably don't love me any more, but…'

'Gio, be quiet.' She squeezed him and then looked up. Resting her hand on his cheek, she felt the rough stubble and saw the tired smudges under his eyes she hadn't noticed before. 'Love doesn't work like that. I couldn't stop loving you even when I wanted to. And believe me, I gave it a really good try.'

The realisation that now she wouldn't have to brought with it a surge of euphoria.

'I'll give you another chance,' she said, knowing all her hopes and dreams were written on her face, 'as long as you promise not to shut me out ever again.'

'You've got your promise,' he said, kissing her. But then he pulled back, framed her face, his eyes shadowed. 'Wait a minute—don't you want me to say I love you back?'

She almost laughed at the look of bewilderment on his face. 'When you're able to do that, that will be lovely.' And she knew he would be able to one day— once he'd become completely secure in the knowledge that she meant everything she said. 'And my romantic heart will cherish the moment. But in the end they're just words, Gio. What really matters is how you feel. And whether you want to be with me and make a commitment that matters.'

Ten years ago she would have demanded he say the words. But she wasn't going to pressure him into it now. He'd come such a long way already.

'That's really noble of you, Issy,' he said, the amusement in his eyes puzzling her. 'But it may surprise you to know I'm not that much of a coward. Not any more.'

'I know,' she replied, not sure where this was leading. To her surprise, he took a step back and got down on one knee. 'What are you doing?'

'Be quiet and let me do this properly.'

'But I told you, it's not necessary.'

'I know what you told me,' he said, his lips quirking as he squeezed her hands tight. 'And you probably even believe it at the moment. Because you're sweet and generous and you never think anything through before you open your mouth.'

'Gee, thanks,' she said, pretty sure that wasn't a compliment.

'Stop pouting and let me say what I've got to say,' he said, his voice sobering. 'Maybe you don't need to hear the words, but I sure as hell need to say them. I owe you this, Issy—for what I said to you ten years ago, and for the things I said a fortnight ago.' He cleared his throat, took a deep breath. 'So here goes.' His eyes fixed on her face as excitement geysered up her chest and made her knees tremble.

'*Ti amo*, Isadora Helligan. I love your sassy wit, the smell of your hair, the feel of your body next to mine when I wake up in the morning. I love that you are always ready to fight for what you think is right and you never back down. I love your passion for life and your spontaneity, and I especially love that drama queen tendency that makes you so damn easy to tease.'

'Hey!' she said, grinning like a fool.

'But most of all, Issy,' he continued, chuckling at her mock outrage, 'I love your courage and your tenacity and your ability to always see the best in people, and that because of all those qualities you gave me all the chances I needed till I finally got it right.'

She flung her arms around his shoulders, almost toppling him over. 'I love you, Gio. So much I'm not even going to make you pay for that drama queen comment.'

He laughed, standing up with her arms still wrapped around his neck. Holding onto her waist, he lifted her easily off the ground, then kissed her with the passion and purpose she adored.

Setting her down at last, he held her face in his hand, brushed a thumb over the tears of joy rolling down her cheeks. 'Don't cry, Issy. This is where the fun starts.'

She smiled up at him, her body quivering with need as his hand stroked under her T-shirt.

'Is that a promise, Hamilton?' she said, lifting a co-quettish eyebrow.

'Pay attention, Helligan,' He hugged her close, his lips hovering above hers. 'That's not a promise, it's a guarantee.'

And then he proved it—in the most delicious way possible.

EPILOGUE

'I MAY have to hate you.' Sophia smiled cheekily as she settled beside Issy on one of the comfortable upholstered chairs that had been set out among the olives groves. 'How did you get your figure back so quickly?'

Issy smiled, weary but blissfully happy. It had been a very long day—she and Gio had been woken up at three that morning by their baby son—but she wouldn't have missed a moment of it. 'Are you joking?' she scoffed. 'Haven't you noticed? My boobs are the size of two small hot-air balloons!'

Sophia laughed. 'Hasn't anyone ever told you? Here in Italy, big is beautiful.'

Colour rose to Issy's cheeks as she spotted Gio making his way towards them across the makeshift dance floor. The loose languid gait she adored made even more beguiling by the tiny baby perched on his shoulder.

'Aha!' Sophia said. 'Someone *has* told you, I think.'

Issy didn't even attempt to hide the blush as her smile spread.

'Someone may have mentioned it,' she replied demurely, enjoying Sophia's delighted giggle as she watched her husband being stopped and kissed by an elderly woman whose name she couldn't remember. There had to be at least a hundred people gathered at the Lorenzo farm to celebrate their son's birth—and even with her greatly improved skill in Italian she was struggling to keep all the names and faces and family connections straight.

As she observed Gio, he took the baby off his shoulder to show him off to the cooing lady, and Issy's grin grew. All the anxiety and confusion of their first visit a year ago had gone. Gio had been relaxed and completely comfortable today—and she suspected it was mostly their son's doing.

One more thing to thank little Marco Lorenzo Hamilton for, whose unexpected arrival had deepened and strengthened their relationship in ways she could never have imagined.

To think she'd agonised for weeks about how to break the news to Gio when she'd fallen pregnant ten months before. Their relationship then had seemed so precious, and yet so vulnerable.

Neither of them had spoken about children since that first early pregnancy scare, and, as much as Issy might have fantasised about having Gio's baby, the abstract romantic dream had swiftly turned into a downward spiral of doubt and panic when that little pink plus sign had appeared in the window of the home pregnancy test.

How would Gio respond to the prospect of becoming a father? How could she ask him to make more changes in his life when he'd already made so many? And how would they both cope with adding yet more pressure to an already difficult domestic situation?

For, once the romance of that mutual declaration of love had worn off, they'd soon discovered that living together was a logistical nightmare. They both had homes they loved and careers they were passionate about in two different cities, hundreds of miles apart.

To solve the problem Gio had insisted on buying a penthouse apartment in Islington, and flying between the two cities three or four times a week. But the long hours Issy put in at the theatre and the nights Gio was forced to spend in Italy meant that even with the exhausting commute they had hardly any quality time together.

Which was how she had managed to get pregnant in the first place, Issy thought wryly, her face flushing as she recalled the many frantic and shockingly explosive encounters they'd snatched together, often in the most preposterous places. She still hadn't quite worked out how she was going to tell her son, if he ever asked, that he had been conceived on the stage of the Crown and Feathers's Theatre Pub late one night after Gio had flown back unexpectedly from Florence and caught her as she locked up.

In the end she would have waited a lot longer to tell Gio about the pregnancy than just a couple of weeks. She'd still been trying to second-guess his reaction and formulate a viable strategy when morning sickness had struck with a vengeance, exactly a month into her pregnancy.

Gio had patted her back while she retched. Made her nibble some dry toast and sip peppermint tea and then insisted she sit down. He had something to tell her. To her total shock he'd announced that they were getting married. That he'd planned to wait until she told him about the baby, but that he couldn't wait any longer. And that he knew the reason she hadn't told him was because she thought he would make a terrible father, but it was way too damn late to worry about that now.

Issy had promptly burst into tears, feeling miserably guilty and totally ecstatic and extremely hormonal—all at the same time. When she'd finally got over her crying jag she'd accepted his proposal, apologised for being such a ninny, and told him she'd never doubted his abilities as a father.

She'd seen he didn't believe her, and it had crucified her, but in the months that had followed the agonising guilt had faded as their relationship changed and developed in new and exciting ways.

Their marriage had been immediate, at Gio's insistence, and necessarily low-key, but still impossibly romantic to Issy's mind. They'd said their vows together one wintry afternoon at Islington Town Hall, with only Issy's mum, Edie, in attendance and had been thrown a surprise reception party by Maxi and the gang at the Crown and Feathers. The baby's first ultrasound scan the day before had only added to the magic of the evening's festivities. Issy had watched, dizzy with happiness, every time Gio whipped out the scan photo—which had looked to her very much like a picture of a large prawn—and showed it to anyone who stood still long enough.

No longer prepared to commute, Gio had announced two days after the wedding that he was relocating his architectural practice to London. The announcement had caused their first major row as husband and wife—because Issy had refused point-blank to let Gio do such an idiotic thing, explaining that *she* was giving up her job at the theatre instead and moving to Florence.

Gio had huffed and puffed, then cajoled and shouted, and eventually sulked for over a week. But Issy had got her way in the end—and enjoyed every minute of his irritation and anger and exasperation.

Gio had been prepared to give up everything for her, and, even though she hadn't been consciously aware of her doubts, when he'd blithely informed her he was moving to London those last nagging doubts about his commitment to their life together had disappeared.

Once he'd informed her of his plans in that matter-of-fact way, and the more strenuously he'd tried to convince her it was the right thing to do, the more Issy had known it wasn't. Her body was ripening more each day with their child, the weight of his ring on her finger made her feel content and secure, and she could see the enthusiasm and excitement on his face when he kissed her growing bump each morning and wished their baby *buongiorno*.

The time was right to give up one dream and concentrate on another.

The ease with which she'd handed over control of the theatre to Maxi and supervised the move to Florence had confirmed her decision. And then to top it all had been that heady rush of love when the Ferrari had pulled up outside her new home and Gio had insisted on carrying her over the threshold—even though she knew she weighed more than a small semi-detached house.

They had begun an ever more exciting phase of their lives as they'd spent those last two months together waiting for the baby's arrival. And she hadn't had a single regret about what she'd left behind.

Not that she had left it entirely behind. She'd kept in touch with Maxi and the gang, and she'd even found some voluntary work at a small children's theatre in the Oltarno before she'd got too huge to move.

But she was more than happy to put her career on hold for now, and enjoy the fruits of her labour. Watching Gio blossom into a warm, loving and ludicrously proud papa had been the sweet, gooey icing on a very large cake. The last of the barriers had dropped away, the last of his insecurities had disappeared. He hadn't just given his whole heart to her and their son, but also to his huge extended family. And being there to witness his transformation had been so intoxicating Issy could feel tears stinging her eyes even now as she observed him chatting easily with the old woman he'd never met before today—as comfortable and relaxed in her company as if he'd known her for years.

She sighed, contentment settling over her like a warm blanket. They both had a place to belong and a future so bright with exciting challenges it was hard not to want to rush to the next one.

As Gio approached, having bade goodbye to his latest friend, Sophia bounced up and kissed him on both cheeks.

'So, how is the proud father holding up?' she asked.

'I'm exhausted.' He sent his cousin a quelling look. 'Next time you and your father and my wife concoct one of these "little get-togethers" my son and I are going to demand full disclosure of the numbers involved.'

Sophia gave an impish giggle. 'Stop pretending you haven't enjoyed showing off your *bambino*,' she said, brushing her hand down the baby's downy black curls. 'I've never seen a man's chest puff up so much.'

The *bambino* in question gave a tired little cry and began to wriggle in Gio's arms. Feeling the instinctive dragging sensation in her breasts, Issy knew what the problem was. She reached for her son. 'How's he holding up to being adored?'

Gio lifted the baby off his shoulder, and kissed his son's cheek before passing him over.

'He's been a superstar. He didn't even grumble when Uncle Carlo lectured him about the intricacies of olive oil production and the importance of carrying on the family tradition.'

Both women laughed.

'Don't panic, Gio,' Sophia said. 'My father has been giving that speech to every baby born in the last forty years. So far only Carmine's son Donato has fallen for it.'

Issy settled back into the chair and eased her breast out of the nursing bra. The baby latched on to the nipple like an Exocet missile and began sucking voraciously.

Sophia patted the baby's head. 'I should find my own *bambino*, before Aldo comes looking for me.' She leaned down to kiss Issy's cheek, then gave Gio a hard hug. 'If I don't catch you later, we'll see you next month for Gabriella's first Holy Communion, yes?'

Gio nodded. 'Wouldn't miss it for the world,' he said, and meant it as he watched his cousin leave. Who would have thought that one day he'd actually be looking forward to these insane gatherings?

He sat beside his wife and child, the feeling of pleasure and contentment and pride that had been building all day making his throat burn. Slinging his arm over the back of Issy's chair, he played with the ends of her hair. Staring at his young son feasting on her lush breast in the gathering twilight he wondered, not for the first time in the last year, how the hell he had ever got so lucky.

'Slow down, fella,' he murmured as the baby's cheeks flexed frantically. 'Anyone would think you hadn't been fed in months.'

'Your uncle Carmine calls it the Italian appetite for life,' Issy said, her throaty giggle sending heat arrowing down to Gio's groin.

He shifted in his seat to ease the pressure, and brushed the curtain of hair behind her ear so he could see her face. 'That sounds like the sort of daft thing Carmine would say. What he means is, our son's greedy.'

Issy turned, her lips curving, and his heart thumped his chest wall. 'Apparently it's a Lorenzo family trait, though, so that's okay,' she said, laughing.

Unable to resist a moment longer, Gio cupped her cheek and touched his lips to hers.

He hadn't meant to be too demanding, hadn't meant to take the kiss any deeper, but when she shuddered and her lips parted his tongue swept into her mouth of its own accord. His hand gripped her head as their mouths fused. He feasted on her, the hunger clawing at his gut like a wild thing.

The little wiggle against his chest and the grumpy little wail had him springing back, so ashamed of himself he felt physically sick.

'Issy, I'm sorry. I don't know what the hell got into me.'

Seeing the look of horror on Gio's face, Issy didn't know whether to laugh, or cry, or scream with frustration. It had been six weeks now since their son's birth. And that brief moment had been their first proper kiss!

'Why are you apologising?' she said, deciding to go

with exasperation as she noticed the large bulge in his loose-fitting suit trousers.

She'd been ready and eager to resume their sex life for weeks now. And she'd seen Gio's almost constant state of arousal recently, so she knew he had to be as frustrated as she was. Still, she'd waited patiently for him to tell her what the problem was. But he hadn't. And her patience had finally run out.

'I want to make love again,' she said, annoyance sharpening her voice. 'And I'm getting a bit tired of you pulling back every time we get intimate.'

His eyebrows rose, and then he frowned. 'I'm being considerate,' he said tightly. 'You've just given birth.'

'I gave birth six weeks ago,' she shot back. 'And I was lucky enough not to need any stitches, so I'm completely healed.'

He paled beneath his tan and winced.

Lifting the now dozing Marco off her breast, Issy readjusted her clothing and placed the baby on her shoulder. She kept her eyes fixed on Gio.

'What exactly is the problem?' she said, her voice rising. 'Are you squeamish about having sex with me because I've had a child? Because if that's the—'

'For God's sake, Issy,' he interrupted, his tone rising to match hers. 'You know perfectly well that's not true. I've been sporting erections Superman would have been proud of in the last month.'

He looked so embarrassed, sounded so frustrated, her bubble of amusement burst out without warning.

'What's so funny?' he asked, his frown deepening.

'Gio,' she said, placing her hand on his cheek as she

tried to stifle the giggles, 'what on earth are you waiting for then?'

His lips quirked. 'Good question.'

Putting his hand on her nape, he rested his forehead on hers, blew out a frustrated breath. 'As much as I love my family, let's sneak out. I'm liable to explode if we have to say goodbye to all these people. And I don't fancy walking around with an erection the size of the Leaning Tower of Pisa while I'm doing it.'

Issy had trouble keeping her mirth under control as they crept furtively through the olive trees to their car. As Gio strapped the sleeping baby into his seat, swearing softly in Italian in his haste, Issy felt desire curl low in her belly and a thrilling surge of heat make her head spin.

Issy rested her palm on her husband's thigh, slid it up seductively as the low-slung car jolted down the rough farm track,

'There's no need to hurry, Gio,' she said, smiling cheekily as his harsh handsome face turned towards her in the shadowy light. 'We've got the rest of our lives.'

He gripped her hand and drew it deliberately off his thigh. 'I know,' he murmured, kissing the tips of her fingers. 'And as soon as we get home I plan to make the most of every single second.'

The cheeky smile turned serene as a rush of love overwhelmed her.

'Well, good.' She sighed. 'That makes two of us, then.'

Coming Next Month

from **Harlequin Presents®**. Available October 26, 2010.

#2951 THE PREGNANCY SHOCK
Lynne Graham
The Drakos Baby

#2952 SOPHIE AND THE SCORCHING SICILIAN
Kim Lawrence
The Balfour Brides

#2953 FALCO: THE DARK GUARDIAN
Sandra Marton
The Orsini Brothers

#2954 CHOSEN BY THE SHEIKH
Kim Lawrence and Lynn Raye Harris

#2955 THE SABBIDES SECRET BABY
Jacqueline Baird

#2956 CASTELLANO'S MISTRESS OF REVENGE
Melanie Milburne

Coming Next Month

from **Harlequin Presents®** EXTRA. Available November 9, 2010.

#125 SHAMEFUL SECRET, SHOTGUN WEDDING
Sharon Kendrick
Snowkissed and Seduced

#126 THE TWELVE NIGHTS OF CHRISTMAS
Sarah Morgan
Snowkissed and Seduced

#127 EVERY GIRL'S SECRET FANTASY
Robyn Grady
Rogues & Rebels

#128 UNTAMEABLE ROGUE
Kelly Hunter
Rogues & Rebels

HPECNM1010

LARGER-PRINT BOOKS!

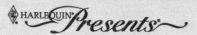

GET 2 FREE LARGER-PRINT NOVELS PLUS 2 FREE GIFTS!

Se~ below for a sneak peek from
our inspirational line, Love Inspired® Suspense

Enjoy this heart-stopping excerpt from
RUNNING BLIND
by top author Shirlee McCoy,
available November 2010!

**The mission trip to Mexico was supposed to be an
adventure. But the thrill turns sour when Jenna Dougherty
and her roommate Magdalena are kidnapped.**

"It's okay. I'm here to help." The voice was as deep as the
darkness, but Jenna Dougherty didn't believe the lie. She
could do nothing but lie still as hands slid down her arms,
felt the rope around her wrists.

"I'm going to use a knife to cut you free, Jenna. Hold
still."

The cold blade of a knife pressed close to her head before
her gag fell away.

"I—" she started, but her mouth was dry, and she could
do nothing but suck in air.

"Shhh. Whatever needs to be said can be said when
we're out of here." Nick spoke quietly, his hand gentle on
her cheek. There and gone as he sliced through the ropes on
her wrists and ankles.

He pulled her upright. "Come on. We may be on
borrowed time."

"I can't leave my friend," Jenna rasped out.

"There's no one here. Just us."

"She has to be here." Jenna took a step away.

"There's no one here. Let's go before that changes."

"It's dark. Maybe if we find a light…"

"What did you say?"

"We need to turn on the light. I can't leave until I know that—"

"What can you see, Jenna?"

"Nothing."

"No shadows? No light?"

"No."

"It's broad daylight. There's light spilling in from the window I climbed in through. You can't see it?"

She went cold at his words.

"I can't see anything."

"You've got a nasty bruise on your forehead. Maybe that has something to do with it." His fingers traced the tender flesh on her forehead.

"It doesn't matter *how* it happened. I'm blind!"

Can Nick help Jenna find her friend or will chasing this trail have Jenna running blindly again into danger?

Find out in RUNNING BLIND, available in November 2010 only from Love Inspired Suspense.